BRANWELL

& Other Stories

By
Michael Yates

Nettle Books

Published 2013 by Nettle Books, Yorkshire
www.nettlebooks.weebly.com
nettlebooks@hotmail.co.uk

©2013 Michael Yates
ISBN: 978-0-9561513-4-6
Classification: Fiction

This book is dedicated to my theatrical partners in crime over the last six years: Helen Shay, Colin Lewisohn and Marian Mantovani.

Contents

The Awkward Squad

THIS BOOK features the Awkward Squad – stories that have never seen the light of day in magazine or anthology.

Some, like *Branwell,* have been produced as stage plays. *The Bronte Boy* toured West Yorkshire, and won Best Actor award for Warwick St John at Wakefield Drama Festival in 2011. Then a new production was commissioned by The Bronte Society for their international AGM weekend this year. My son suggested I turn it into a novel, but I didn't have the stamina to add an extra 50,000 words. So here it is in the half-way house of the *novella*; where, to my surprise, it seems to be a happy lodger.

The Navigator's Daughter also played as a drama in Yorkshire theatres. As did *Till My Eyes Bleed,* performed in Wakefield and Leeds and at Ilkley Literature Festival.

But some stories in this volume never made it to the stage. They were left in literary limbo – too long for a short story, too short for a novel.

The 12,000-word *Priceless!* was written because, in real-life, corrupt Yorkshire architect John Poulson wrote an autobiography, *The Price,* discarded and pulped by his publisher after legal threats. One day a copy of this fugitive book came into my hands. It gave me new insight into his personality. Above all, it gave me his authentic voice. Although this version is obviously fiction, I hope I have captured some of the truth. In contrast, the 10,000-word *Suntdot,* a story about the struggles of a naïve young schoolteacher, is based on my own teaching experiences in a more innocent age. This year is the 50th anniversary of the murder of US President Jack Kennedy; and I have used the excuse to include *Now It Can Be Told,* an obviously imaginative account of how different the world might have been if those bullets had missed their target...

Now, as Charlotte Bronte says of her siblings' novels in *Branwell*: "At least they are out in the world. At least they do not fester at home, as *we* do."

Michael Yates 2013

Branwell

PIANO MUSIC ran through his head as he came down the
stairs. Gentle, soothing music. It was... *Oh, what was it?*
Chopin surely. Probably Chopin. When had he heard it
played? Perhaps in Leeds when his father had taken him...
How long ago was that? *So* long ago.

A voice interrupted the Ballade, for that was most
certainly what it was. The voice was his father's. His father was
standing in the hall, shouting.

He was shouting: "Hear me! You will hear me, sir!"

Branwell reached the bottom stair and shouted back. "I
hear you, sir! I hear you!"

Now his father was upon him. Now his father was
shouting more loudly: "You do *not*, sir! You do not *listen*!"

Branwell swallowed. He must be more controlled. He
must be more quiet. Like Chopin. He said more quietly: "I *listen*,
sir. I listen, father." He hesitated. "Oh father...!" his voice rose
half an octave and he raised his hands as if in prayer. Then they
slumped to his sides of their own accord.

His father was still shouting. His father, whose last name
he shared with his son: Bronte. Whose first name was also his
son's: Patrick. Though everyone called the son Branwell. To
distinguish between father and son. To distinguish between the
distinguished and the *un*distinguished...

His father shouted: "It is noon, sir! Noon! And you are
not yet dressed!"

Branwell looked down to see if it was true. Well, he was
in his dressing gown. He would defend himself. He said: "I am
dressed, sir! I am dressed well enough. For the *house*, sir. For my
study. Well enough for the house." He was pleased how quietly
he spoke.

His father said: "I would help you dress if..."

Now it was Branwell's turn to be angry. Now his voice
rose with his anger. "Sir, I am your son but I am no longer your
child!"

"You are in drink, sir! Look at you!"

5

"I have had a glass, father. That is all." Had he started shouting? He would speak more quietly. Like the Chopin. But the Chopin had gone out of his head. He said more quietly: "And I have looked in that glass. I have seen my face, sir. I know my face!" He wondered why he was saying that.

His father said: "There is work to be done." And then more quietly: "There is always work."

"I do my work, father. I work." Was this quiet enough? Would it impress his father? Would it prevent his father from shouting again? "Even now," Branwell went on, "I return to it. I return to my desk." Was this true? Yes, it was. He really was about to re-enter the study. He was about to go back to his work. He had spoken truly.

His father said: "Well then, I shall be pleased to see it. When it is finished. Whatever your work may be." His father turned and walked vigorously towards the front door and through it into the garden and the graveyard beyond. Making his rounds in the village perhaps. He always had rounds. He always had visits. He always had things to do and things to say. People always listened to Branwell's father.

Branwell spoke. Again he spoke quietly. Though there was no longer anyone to hear. "Finished," he said, "Finished. Oh, Father. Our father..." Then he made up his mind. Yes, he *would* go to his desk. "Father, I go to my desk. I go to my work. I go now!"

BRANWELL GLANCED round the study as though fearful it might have changed in his short absence. But no. There was the desk, the darkness of its oak hidden as always by the plethora of paper. On the desk as well as the paper was a cut-glass decanter still half full of clear liquid, a small glass bottle with a blue tint to it, a quill pen in its silver ink well, a ball of sealing wax, and a spirit glass not thoroughly washed. Behind the desk was his high-backed chair with a red plush seat, now rather worn. Leaning against the legs of the chair were three paintings, their backs to him. Branwell walked across to the desk and picked up a sheet of paper at random.

He read – though he was not quite sure whether he did so aloud: "To the editor, Blackwoods Magazine. Sir, read what I write. If it please you." He hesitated. Read what I have *written*? Write? Written? *Have* written? Yes. He picked up the quill and made the correction. "Sir, read what I have written. If it please you. I have addressed you twice before and now I do so yet again." He glanced up at the ceiling. "Oh, let it please you. Oh God, oh Father, let it please the editor." He continued to read. "I have attached a poem of my own devising, which the editor of the *Halifax Guardian* has seen fit to print this last month. The *Halifax Guardian* is a most learned and respectable newspaper within the county of Yorkshire."

He pondered. What would they think now it was already published? Would they think it used and stale? He wrote quickly: "I trust, sir, that you will not think it used and stale that it has already been published, for the *Halifax Guardian* is seldom read beyond the bounds of Halifax itself." He stopped. He put the pen back in the ink well. *No, no!* He dropped the paper back on the desk but it fluttered to the floor.

"We shall start again, Mr Editor." He picked it up, then again picked up the pen. "A new paragraph, a new sentence, sir." He was suddenly aware of the decanter as though it had moved of its own accord into the vista of his gaze. He stretched out his pen hand and touched it. "That I might drink and leave the world unseen, Mr Keats." He caught himself and withdrew his hand. Then he dropped the letter back on the desk. "The Royal Academy! The Royal Academy! I had already begun a new epistle…"

He searched through the papers. "Oh where..? Where..? Ah!" He picked it up. Yes, yes! He read: "The Secretary, The Royal Academy. Sir, you will recall this is not the first time I have written to you." He paused. Wrote. *Have* written. Yes. *Have written*! Leave it. He read: "We had arranged an appointment and I was to bring you some of my paintings, half a dozen small watercolours which I consider bear comparison with the early works of Mr Turner; and which my friends, all learned men hereabout, had said were not without merit." He felt suddenly discomfited. "I also planned to bring two larger oil paintings which my friends and family had also enjoyed and over which the name of Mr Gainsborough was frequently invoked. By so doing, I had been hoping to forego some of the formal examination procedure which is customary with you." He stopped, put the paper down on the desk, slumped back into the high-backed chair, put his head in his hands.

After a minute, he leaned across to the paintings, moved the largest to one side so he might see it more clearly, then put it back. He picked up the letter and read: "But alas, when the scheduled day came, I was, I regret to say, inconvenienced." But would that do? No, no! He crossed out *inconvenienced* and wrote *obstructed*. "Obstructed by some family business which was wholly unforeseen. I trust, sir that you will allow me to make amends, even at this late hour, by admitting me to a further appointment. I am still able to bring you the oil paintings which, by happy coincidence, are still unsold despite my having begun a thriving portraiture establishment in Bradford. The paintings are first, of my sisters, of which I have three remaining." Would they know what he meant by that? He wrote: "That is, three *paintings*. Though, as it happens, I also have three sisters." He stopped and thought: *To tell truth, I have very many paintings remaining.* He read: "And second I can bring you a depiction of the countryside near Haworth rectory which is our home." He stopped reading and again touched the decanter with his pen hand. He thought: I tried to do one of *you*, father, but I couldn't catch the likeness. He wondered if he had said *that* aloud.

He put down the pen and paper, grasped the decanter and poured some of the liquid into his glass. He looked over the desk. He picked up another sheet. He said: "Now. What is this?" But he knew what it was. He read: "To the Directors, the Leeds and Manchester Railroad. Dear Sirs, I write to bring to your attention a very grave injustice. Some years ago, I served as an employee of your company at the Sowerby Bridge Railway station. During my term of duty, a sum of money…"

He scrunched up the paper and dropped it on the floor. He took a drink from the glass and refilled it. He looked hard at the decanter. He put down the glass. Hurriedly now, he pulled open one of the drawers and took out a fresh sheet. He wrote: *John Brown, Sexton of the Parish. Friend John, My spirits are low. I shall feel very much obliged if you can contrive to bring me five pence worth of gin in a proper measure. I could perhaps*

*take it from you at the lane top when I shall imburse you. I shall
get this letter to you in the usual way.*

He folded the paper and wrote John's name on it. He
raised his glass. He said: "One glass. That's all I have had today,
Mr Editor, Mr Secretary, Mr Gainsborough, Mr Railway
Director..." At each name he raised the glass and took another
sip. He said: "Mr Reverend Bronte!" But he had already drained
the glass. He put it down.

He looked across at the small bottle with the bluish tint.
A medicine bottle. He said: "A draught or two of laudanum." He
picked it up, pulled the cork and sipped from it. "Well, I have a
cold. It's good for me." Now he *knew* he was talking aloud.
"Emily takes it regularly. Charlotte used to. And that friend of
hers. That Gaskell woman. Takes it all the time. Only thing is: it
does make you sleepy. It makes you dream."

He leaned across the desk and rested his head on his
arms.

LITTLE CHARLOTTE was pummelling his shoulder, shouting
at him: "Brother, brother, be awake!"

He was drowsy. All he could say was: "What?"

"I want to play! I want to play!"

She ran back across the room, to the table covered with
the blue and white cotton cloth their Aunt had brought when she
first came to stay and look after them. Charlotte grasped the
hobby horse propped up in the recess, pulled up her apron and
thrust the horse beneath her skirts. Branwell felt the thrill of the
chase. He pulled off his dressing gown. He found, to his surprise,
that he was wearing the tunic of an English grenadier. He leapt to
his feet and ran after her.

Round and round the table, then he caught her and
hugged her. "Charlotte! Charlotte! Yes, I'll play. But not *girls'*
games! Not games that *girls* play!"

Charlotte turned. She waved the horse's head at him. "*I*
do not play girls' games!"

"No, you don't!" he had to admit it. "Allright then!
We'll play war!"

Charlotte let go of the horse so it fell over. She clapped
her hands. "*La guerre*!" she shouted.

9

Branwell made a face. "Is that French? I do not like French."

"You do not like French because you do not know any."

He thought about it. "I do not care to learn it. It is not a *man's* language. Not like English. I think is the lack of consonants spoils it for a man."

Charlotte laughed. "I *love* French. But then, I suppose I am a girl!"

"But you like war!" He had to give her that. He had to give Charlotte her due.

"Oh yes! I do! We'll have battles and massacres and carnage! I love carnage!"

"I am glad. For I do tend to write carnage. When I am in the mood." He ran back to his desk and opened one of the drawers. He pulled out his tiny exercise book. "Look," he said, "It is all here." He opened the book. "I have worked very hard on it. I trust you will find as much carnage as your heart may desire!"

"Oh, I'm sure I shall," said Charlotte, then: "What is the story?" She ran across to him.

Branwell thumbed through the book and found the place. "This is a great day for the Glasstown Confederacy!"

Charlotte clapped her hands again and began to skip. "Oh yes! Oh yes!" Then she caught herself. "Why?"

"Because they are poised to conquer the whole of the nation of Angria in the name of King Zamorna and raise their banner amongst the African natives, of course. And when they have done so, why! There will be other lands and other worlds to conquer. For Angria, once a backward and pagan state, shall take its rightful place among the powerful nations of the earth."

That seemed to impress her. "Bravo!" And then she said something very girlish. "And is there love in the story?"

Branwell was... oh, what was the word? Nonplussed. "Love? Why should there be love?"

Charlotte gave him her superior look but he could see she was not as sure of herself as she pretended. "There is always love, otherwise what will the soldiers do when they have won?" She looked embarrassed. "They must have something to do when the battle is over."

Branwell thought about it. "Well, I suppose they will celebrate."

"How?"

"With feasts. As you find in Mr Shakespeare. In Macbeth, for example."

"And dancing?" Charlotte pirouetted, her skirts swirling high around her. "Will there be dancing? As you find in Miss Austen?"

Branwell was shocked. "You are reading Miss Austen?"

Charlotte hesitated. "Only when I am tired. Or I have a headache."

Branwell snorted. It was a good snort. He repeated it. "It would require a very large headache to induce *me* to read Miss Austen. Why, there are no massacres, no carnage..."

Charlotte looked down at her feet. She moved quite close to him. "It is true I *do* enjoy carnage, but in its proper place." She paused. "Now, where are the soldiers?"

"You know where the soldiers are. In their box. Where they *always* are."

"Then you must let them out!" Charlotte ran ahead and he thought for a moment she would pull open the drawer. But she held back. "You're good at letting out the soldiers."

Branwell put down the exercise book and moved towards her. He could smell the soapy clean little girl smell of her. He opened the drawer very slowly and took out the wooden box, opened it and extracted three English soldiers in bright red uniforms.

Charlotte pointed to the one with the rifle at his shoulder. "That young one there is very handsome!"

Branwell did not normally think of soldiers as handsome but he decided to appease her. "It is his uniform makes him so. Sometimes I think we should all wear uniforms. Everyone should be known for what he is – a colonel, a lieutenant, a private."

"And for what *she* is."

"Don't be silly." He raised his voice. "You don't have girls in the army."

But Charlotte was adamant. "I'm sure you do. I read somewhere about some women who were camp followers."

Branwell carried the soldiers and their box over to the table and spilled them out on the cloth. "Well, it was probably like the song when Sweet Polly Oliver followed her sweetheart to the wars. But she only *dressed* as a soldier. She wasn't really one of them."

"But it's the uniform that matters. That's what you said."

He felt caught out. He would not have it. "Except when it comes to *girls*!"

But she was no longer interested in the argument. "That one there." She pointed. "He looks a bit like father."

"Right. He can be the general. General Percy."

"But he's not got a general's uniform."

"If he's father, then he'll be the general."

"But that's not what you said!" It seemed for a moment she might cry. But then she caught herself. "Oh. Allright."

By now there were a half-a-dozen red-clad soldiers sprawled on the cloth and another half-dozen in various colours to denote the French and other enemies. Branwell helped the soldiers to their feet. "The redoubtable General Percy is very important. For when King Zamorna has gained his victories, I think General Percy will plot against him. I think they may be rivals for domination." He said: "Where is the artillery? Where are the big guns?" But they had only ever had one big gun and it had been trampled on and broken by their Aunt.

Charlotte had grown quiet. Then: "Dear brother, do not take this amiss but..." She paused. "You said *poised*. Poised to conquer. That's what you said. Sometimes it is not enough to be poised. Perhaps something untoward will happen..."

He shook his head. "Something untoward? Never!"

She said: "Perhaps..."

"No. Never. They have proved their mettle, they have proved their..."

"Their steel!" she interrupted.

Branwell was suddenly annoyed. "No, Charlotte. When I say they have proved their mettle, I spell it differently. It is the word *mettle* meaning courage and ardent temperament, not the word *metal* meaning an elementary substance such as gold or iron or tin."

She said: "You are so clever, Branwell," but he wondered if she were making a fool of him, "You are so grown-up. You sometimes make me forget I am the elder by a good twelve-month."

"It is because I am a boy. Boys have larger brains. Well, if we can't find the artillery it will have to be hand-to-hand."

Now he picked up two of the English soldiers and smashed them against four of the enemy in turn. He made little explosions in the back of his throat.

Charlotte held out her hand. "Let me have father!"

He pulled back, holding tight to the rifleman but accidentally dropping the drummer boy. "Why?"

"Hand-to-hand is extremely taxing on the constitution. And father is a person of sedentary pursuits, unused to the African climate."

Branwell laughed. Though it came out more high-pitched than he had intended. "He is a man! And hand-to-hand is no sacrifice for such as he, who has risen to the rank of general."

Charlotte still held out her hand. She would not be satisfied. "I do not want him to be a casualty. I do not want him to partake of the carnage. I do not want him to die or be in any way posthumous!"

There was a sudden silence between them. Almost like a grown-up silence. Branwell looked across to the window, bright with the brave but uncertain sunlight of spring. Then he looked back at the table top, mostly in shadow. Still she stood with her hand towards him, towards the rifleman who was Father. Eventually he said: "He will not die. Has Father not proved himself? Has he not outlived so many others in this war?"

"Maria," said Charlotte.

"Elizabeth," Branwell joined the incantation.

"Our sisters."

"And our mother."

"Our household…"

Household stirred resistance in Branwell. He said: "Household *cavalry*. Why do we have no cavalry?" He began again to smash the red soldiers against the others. Then: "Look. Perhaps he will be wounded. General Percy will be wounded. Wounded only!"

"Oh no!" Charlotte would not be mollified.

"He will not die."

"He *must* not!"

In a moment Branwell had decided. "You will nurse him back to health."

But it did not bring her reassurance. "Will he be wounded for long?"

It was a foolish question. "Not if you nurse him well. Not if we choose it differently."

Charlotte sighed. "Then let us choose it differently. I would not want to spend my life nursing father."

There was another grown-up silence. Branwell broke it. "You know, perhaps there *might* be dancing. A ball perhaps. If the officers wished."

Charlotte's face grew bright again. "It will be a chance for the officers to while away their time during the peace."

"There will not be peace for long. It is not the way of things."

"It can be for a short time." Charlotte looked almost wheedling. "A ball does not take up more than a short time. It is a necessary thing that officers should meet young ladies. And the king of Angria should meet them too."

Somehow he had been wrong-footed. He said: "Why the king? Why King Zamorna, the great warrior of Angria?"

For once, Charlotte looked almost scornful. It was not an expression he enjoyed. She said: "Why, kings even more than officers. For kings must have sons to occupy their thrones after them."

She had won the point and he would have to acknowledge it. "Very well. Then Zamorna, the mighty warrior of Angria, shall marry." He considered the obvious candidate. "He shall marry Mary, the daughter of General Percy."

Charlotte considered. "But King Zamorna and General Percy do not seem well-matched. You said yourself they are secret rivals in the struggle for domination."

He nodded. "That is what I am writing in my *History of Angria*."

"Of course, if King Zamorna and Miss Percy love each other truly, then no-one should stand in their way."

"General Percy will see that this is his chance of winning favour with Zamorna. And Zamorna will see that it is his way of controlling General Percy. He will make General Percy his Prime Minister."

"And will that lead to another war?"

"Of course."

"Even though they are become the same family?"

Branwell sighed. Did girls understand nothing? "It is always so with great families that they should wage war and kill each other. Consider. Richard III and the Duke of Clarence were brothers." He thought about it "I must write this down." He rushed back to his desk, picked up a pen and his exercise book.

But Charlotte was moody. "I am grown bored with this. I do not want the family to kill each other."

"It is only what you get in Sir Walter Scott. The Highland Clans. I thought you *liked* Sir Walter."

Charlotte turned away. "I am now less for Sir Walter and more for Lord Byron."

"You told me you *adored* Sir Walter. Sir Walter is a man who knows his battles and his soldiery. Why should you change? What faults do you now perceive in Sir Walter?"

Charlotte thought about it. "Perhaps he is too Scotch. I do not know. About Lord Byron, there is something, well, I cannot say what kind of something, but it is not at all *Scotch*." She gazed up to the heavens.

Branwell decided to tease her. "And yet I believe there is some Scotchness in him."

"Then," said Charlotte, "he has hid it well."

There was another brief silence. Then from Charlotte: "Will General Percy really go to war against King Zamorna?"

"It is inevitable."

"But they have so much in common. A woman who loves them both…" Charlotte, Branwell noted, was near to tears.

"It is destiny. For a woman, love is destiny. For a man…"

"What is it for a man?"

"To be something in the world. To be…" He could not find the words. "A girl would not understand it."

Charlotte looked strangely coy. "I think perhaps I do. I think perhaps it is found somewhat in Byron."

Suddenly: their father's voice. It was raised, looking for its audience. "Children! Children! Where are you?"

Charlotte cried: "Father! It's Father! Quick! Put the soldiers away! Keep them safe!"

"You cannot keep soldiers safe. It is not in their nature."

They put the soldiers back in the box and the box back in the drawer. And the exercise book. Charlotte smoothed her apron.

Branwell said: "Come. Let us speak with our father."

"With the redoubtable General Percy," said Charlotte, and they went off skipping. They left the hobby horse to make its own way.

PATRICK WAS in the hall shouting. "Children! Children! Where are you? Branwell! Charlotte! Emily! Anne! Come to me! Come! Here!" When they did so, arriving raggedly from their drawing, writing and divers housework, Emily still carried the besom. They saw he held a letter and was waving it. They looked at each other. They looked at him. They laughed and squealed. Emily nearly dropped her broom.

"Work!" shouted Patrick in approval, "There is always work! But always the works of the Almighty are great and good! And today, under his guidance, our own work has come to fruition! I have here a letter..." he waved it about once more "...from..." he allowed himself pause "...The Royal Academy!"

There was a general intake of breath then some cheering, awkward at first. Patrick waved his hands to encourage them. The cheering became louder. He gestured with his hands to end it.

In the silence he said: "Branwell, I have taken the liberty of opening this missive, though it is clearly addressed to you."

Branwell, who was by now just as tall as his father, said: "I forgive you, Father." He put out his hand to take it but his father held it back.

Patrick said: "Branwell has been offered an interview with the Royal Academy for a place among their students." He allowed them to see his delight. "He is to meet with the secretary

16

on the second of next month. *All their works they do to be seen of men. Matthew 23.*" Only then did he hand the letter to Branwell.

Branwell took his time reading it. "There is still an examination, father, a procedure to be followed, before I can be taught there."

"But for one like yourself, my son, I fully expect it will be waived. You have much to show them…"

"I have a few paintings of some worth…" Branwell was nervous.

"Oh they are *brilliant!*" shouted Anne, "You are brilliant, Branwell!"

Patrick nodded. "Thank you, Anne."

"He will be such a success, will he not, father?"

"I believe he will, Emily. He has been well taught, I know, by my friend Mr Williams in his studio in Leeds."

"And I have tried, sir," said Branwell, "to copy from nature."

"We have *all of us* tried to copy from nature," said Charlotte, "We have all, I believe, reached a certain dexterity with the sketching pencil."

Patrick nodded. "Dexterity. It is no more than I should expect of my family. *Everyman's work shall be made manifest. Corinthians Chapter 3.*"

"And every *woman's?*"

Patrick ignored Charlotte. He was gazing at Branwell. "My children are olive branches round my table, but there is one will grow like a cedar in Lebanon."

"But supposing he falls?" Emily again.

Patrick showed his annoyance. "He does not fall."

"He *used to fall*, father. All the time." This from Anne.

"That was many years ago, daughters. And it was not *all* the time. It was a thing of childhood. It was grown out of."

Charlotte broke the ensuing silence. "If it is to be the second of the month, father, when Branwell must go forth…"

"…to the Royal Academy!" Patrick laughed. His good humour was restored.

"Father, there are great preparations to be made. And precious little time."

17

"Yes, yes, Charlotte. Shirts to be washed, bread to be baked, pictures to be framed, tickets to be bought. I rely on you to organise the details. And I say to the rest of my family: *Do as Charlotte tells you.* It is a great adventure for all of us and we must all play our part."

He put his hand on Branwell's shoulder. Branwell said: "A few paintings of some worth." He sounded timid.

"*For to be seen of men,*" said Patrick.

"And I have tried, sir, to copy from nature."

"*And your work made manifest.*"

"And," said Charlotte, "precious little time!"

"WHOOAAHH!!" YELLED the coachman. Branwell was out of the door before the horses had properly halted. But he landed well. On his feet. With his new top hat clutched firmly in his hand. "Whoaahh!!" yelled the coachman, "Whoa there! Whoa there!"

The coachman helped Branwell haul his luggage down from the top. His beige carpetbag was heavy with his canvases, rolled up and tied with ribbon. They had debated much whether to leave on the frames because there was no doubt that a good frame enhanced a good picture. But Charlotte had pointed out the problems of transporting so much extra weight.

Branwell held his bag in his right hand and with the other picked up the skirts of his greatcoat to keep them clear of the mud. He made his way to the dark-timbered door of The Walnut Tree Inn. Once inside, he emphasised that the room had been properly ordered by Charlotte in a letter more than a week ago.

"Mr Bronte," said the landlord and laughed. He was a fat, bald man with the joviality of his trade.

"The same," said Branwell.

The landlord showed him the room, which was clean and had a goose-feather mattress on the bed. Branwell ordered a meal of Cheddar cheese and plain brown bread because (though he did not own to this) the journey had made him a trifle queasy; anyway, it would be good to conserve what money he had. Then he went downstairs. The low-ceilinged public room was crowded and smoky and his eyes were a little sensitive at the best of times. But he could discern a table at the far end with at least one heavy oak chair vacant. He made for it.

"A jug of something?" asked the landlord, "Spirits?"

Branwell smiled. "I am already in good spirits." And the landlord laughed again.

"WE SHOULD be in good spirits," said Charlotte, "for General Percy will not die. When King Zamorna has gained his victories, I think General Percy will plot against him. I think they may be rivals for domination. But I think neither of them need die." She waved the tiny exercise book that contained Branwell's scrawl of so many years ago.

They were in the study. Charlotte sat on the high-backed chair. Emily was sweeping in a corner of the room. Anne lay languorously across the desk top. She said: "I do not care if they live or die." She giggled and leapt to her feet.

Charlotte was shocked. "Anne! How can you... ?"

Anne was obviously anxious to annoy. "They are not *real,* sister! They are only stories."

Charlotte's face glowed with her anger. "There was a time when you respected King Zamorna and General Percy, when you more readily took part in the great and chivalrous deeds of Angria!" She threw the exercise book down on the desk.

Emily leaned the besom against the wall. "There are other lands and other worlds to explore, Charlotte. Now Anne and I have become pilgrims."

"Yes," said Anne, "pilgrims."

"We have decided," said Emily, "to traverse further afield. We have our own country now where the people listen to us."

"WHY," SAID the voice in the shadow in the corner, "It's Mr Branwell sir! A veritable pilgrim! Of all the folk in the country..."

Branwell was bemused. He screwed up his eyes behind his spectacles. "I do not..." And then he *did* know. "It is Brown, is it not? John Brown?"

The other stepped forward so the light from an oil lamp fell directly on his face. He shook Branwell's hand with enthusiasm. "It is, Mr Branwell. John Brown. Tha father's sexton." He laughed. "Tha father's *gravedigger*."

Branwell also laughed, though awkwardly. "I cannot conceive it! That I should arrive at this very inn in the great metropolis and discover you here!"

"The coach road from Bradford to London is well travelled, sir," said Brown, "If we have made that same journey, even at differing times, it is no surprise we should meet here. Come let us sit together." He indicated the table for which Branwell had been making anyway and they pulled up two chairs and sat down. "What, if I may ask, brings thee to this destination?"

Branwell thought hard before replying. He was never one to boast. In any case, the goal was not quite in his grasp and God might punish him if... He swallowed. He said: "I hope, Brown, that it may be not so much my destination but a mere staging post, if I may use that metaphor..."

"Why, you may, sir. Of course you may. What is a metaphor to a gentleman like yourself? I myself am happy with a metaphor. For we are *all* readers now, sir. We working folk too have our schoolhouses and our libraries."

"Yes, it is a great age we live in!" Branwell agreed, and then the words tumbled out. "I am, as you say, a sort of pilgrim, Brown, and my quest is to stake my claim to be a part of this great age. I have an interview with the Royal Academy. Tomorrow morning, nine o'clock sharp."

"And I'm sure that's what tha'll be, sir. *Sharp* as a butcher's knife. But I too am a pilgrim." Brown looked round nervously, as though fearing eavesdroppers.

Branwell felt suddenly excited. "And what is your quest?"

"Nothing less than the sacred work of the Great Architect of the Universe."

"You mean God?"

"That is not a name I speak lightly, sir. But ay, I *do* mean God. Here. Let me pour a libation."

There were two spirit glasses and a porcelain jug already on the table, though Branwell had not previously noticed. Indeed, they seemed strangely out of place in that room of ale, porter and pewter tankards; but, as Branwell had often mused – and the Romantic poets had proved – life was *often* strange. Brown filled them both.

"THIS IS not a thing I say lightly." Charlotte paused for breath, made a decision to speak more slowly. "I do not know what quest you can pursue in another country, sisters, that you cannot pursue in the perfectly adequate nation founded by Branwell and myself. You should not speak lightly of Angria. Your brother and I have constructed our nation with painstaking detail, that there should be for all of us a land of justice and nobility, a land of..."

"Cannon!" shouted Emily.

"And war!" from Anne.

"And parades!"

"And politics! Ugh!"

Charlotte gritted her teeth. "These are the very things of life. What else can there be?"

"Poetry," replied Anne, "There is no poetry in Angria. Only battle hymns. And speeches. For when people die."

"So we two," said Emily, "have founded an entirely new country. Gondal."

"And what would I find in Gondal, sisters? If I should care to make such an excursion in the first place? Which I *very* much doubt I should!"

Anne waved her arms. "Joy! Ecstasy!"

Emily interrupted her. "Not all the time, it has to be said. For I think it is not wholly proper to require joy and ecstasy *all* the time. But now and again. That is perfectly acceptable. With perhaps a little pain intermingled." She stepped forward and began to declaim:

"Darkness and glory rejoicingly blending,
earth rising to heaven and heaven descending,
man's spirit away from its drear dungeon sending!"

She ended with a pirouette. She was standing very close to Charlotte now. She gazed insolently at her older sister.

Anne burst out laughing. She clapped her hands. "It is good! Is it not good, Emily's poem?"

"Why, yes!" admitted Charlotte, "It is *promising.*"

Emily said: "Only promising?" Her face remained very close to Charlotte's, their noses almost touching.

"More than promising perhaps," said the eldest sister, "But the mood is uncertain. How can darkness and glory rejoicingly blend? No, no. I consider it too metaphysical. And the mood changes are too abrupt. *Drear dungeon*, indeed!"

Emily began to circle Charlotte like some jungle cat they might have read about. Like Blake's *Tyger* perhaps. Then she stepped back and smiled. "Drear dungeon indeed!" she exclaimed in imitation of Charlotte, "But if Branwell had written it…"

"If Branwell had spoken it…" Anne joined in.

"Why, then it would be light as birdsong…" Emily posed like a ballerina with her arms poised above her head.

"…and we should be carried away on the wings of poesy!" Anne waved her arms like a bird's wings.

Charlotte could no longer control her anger. "Do not speak slightingly of your brother! You would not do so if he were here!"

"And where is he?" asked Emily.

"You know only too well…"

"Tell us again!"

"For we are only children," said Anne, "and we are very forgetful!"

Charlotte sighed. But she was pleased to have moved away from Gondal. "You are no longer children," she said, "but young women. Nevertheless, I will tell you once more: Branwell is making his way in the world as we shall all need to do."

"Away from this dreary dungeon!" cried Emily.

JOHN BROWN was pouring another gin. "Free, Mr Branwell. All men free from the dungeon of life. Free to live as brothers. Free to do owt they please if it please the Architect."

22

"Brotherly love? Is that not the teaching of our own Lord Jesus?"

"It is, ay. And we Masons do not deny the Lord Jesus. Nor the Hebrew Lord of Moses. Nor the Lord of the Mohammedans. Nor *any* Lord. But we are, sir, more practical. For that is the nature of God, is it not? He has designed and structured a universe more powerful than the steam engine, more beautiful than the blast furnace, more teeming with life than the backstreets of Manchester, a universe of infinite beauty! And what does he ask of us?

Branwell paused in his drinking. "What?"

"Only that we acknowledge the three great needs of man. First, that we honour and respect each other, every degree and kind and appetite. Though of course, I do not include Papists."

"Why, no! Of *course* not Papists!"

"Second, that we relieve the sufferings of our fellow man as best we can with the methods to hand..." John Brown was refilling Branwell's glass. "And third, that we do not deny each other, whatever we may be, we do not deny our brotherhood. Which is why I am here in this city."

"You come to...?"

"To meet with other Masons, the men of other lodges, to share a glimpse of the divine diagram, if such a phrase is not too high-fangled for a man of my station..."

"No, no, I believe it is not." Branwell was pleased to be having this conversation about the nature of the Infinite, pleased and surprised that he should be having it with a man like Brown in surroundings like The Walnut Tree.

"We have both of us read books, Mr Branwell, from the shelves of the Mechanics' Institute."

"Yes! Yes!"

"We Masons mean to share a glimpse of the whole, of the Grand Design of the Great One. For tha must know, as *we* do, the proportion of Solomon's Temple in Jerusalem was no more than an imitation of the system of the natural world."

"Er...yes. I believe so."

23

"Solomon's temple is the secure foundation on which all our hopes are based. The inner sanctuary alone was 20 cubits long, 20 cubits wide and 20 cubits high."

"Why, yes!"

"The holy building is a symphony. Does tha know the music of the spheres?"

"I…"

"The cube that is the base of the temple is the symbol of all the consonances in music because the ratio of its sides is one-to-one, which represents the note of unison…"

Branwell nodded. "Unison."

"…or the full-string length containing within itself the vibrations of all the other musical intervals. The cube is sacred because its eight corners form the harmonic mean between its six faces and its twelve edges."

Branwell put down his glass. "I must confess I am not so much musical as I am poetic…"

"And the Holy of Holies, with its adjacent chambers, was 20 cubits broad and 30 cubits high. And the nave in front was 40 cubits long. Thus the proportions are 40 x 30 x 20." Brown held out his hands as if somehow to demonstrate. "These ratios are exactly the same as those which mark the musical intervals of the octave. It can therefore be said that the Temple of Solomon expressed the fundamental, the octave, the fifth and the fourth, known as the perfect consonances because they are invariable."

"Invariable!" Now Branwell was excited.

"Ay, tha can believe it."

"I do. I *do*." And yes, he could see it all. "Such is a noble design."

"Humanity itself is invariable, sir. The true nature of humanity is invariable and homogeneous. So no man may feel himself an outcast."

John Brown poured another glass for each of them.

"SISTERS," SAID Charlotte, "do not make yourselves outcasts from the world we have created".

"No, we would never do that. Would we, Emily?"

"I wonder what he does now," said Emily.

"Branwell?" asked Anne.

"Branwell!" said Emily.

"He prepares himself," said Charlotte, "He girds his loins for the battle of the morrow."

Emily and Anne began to giggle, then the fit was altogether upon them and they staggered, lurched, fell into each other, their laughter coming ever faster, louder, more hysterical.

Charlotte bit her lip. It was *her* fault. She should not have used the word *loins*. "Really," she said, "is this how the daughters of Gondal behave? While the Great Son of Angria prepares to shine in the world? To make his mark with study and high-mindedness?"

Emily put a hand to her mouth. She steadied herself. She said: *"All their works they do to be seen of men!"* It was a fair imitation of their father's Irish intonation.

"Everyman's work shall be made manifest!" said Anne.

"And he shall *gird up his loins!"*

Charlotte leapt to her feet. "Enough!" she shouted.

BRANWELL WAS slumped across the table.

"Enough, enough," said John Brown. "Now, now, Mr Branwell, we shall have to get thee to tha room. What was it our Lord Jesus said? Take no thought for the morrow, Mr Branwell. For are we not all accounted in the Draughtsman's Great Design? Does he not see the weakness of our natures and balance them against the rest of His creation? Ay, let us hope He does."

John Brown took hold of Branwell, lifted him from the chair, pulled Branwell's arm across his own broad shoulders. The bald landlord was most understanding. "Young gentleman taken poorly," he said and gave John Brown Branwell's key. John Brown supported Branwell up the stairs.

"Ay, let us hope He does."

HE HAD come into the study knowing something was amiss but unsure what it might be. He knew as soon as he saw his father seated at the desk.

Branwell said: "Father! I see you have…"

" … taken the liberty of opening this missive." He waved the letter. "…from the Leeds and Manchester Railroad Company."

"The Leeds…" began Branwell.

"… and Manchester Railroad Company."

"My employers."

"Your *former* employers."

"Yes."

"Yes, *sir*!"

"Yes, father!"

"They speak of a sum of money…"

"Yes."

"Eleven pounds…"

"…one shilling and sevenpence."

"…one shilling *and seven pence*! You are correct, sir. How I wish you had been correct very much earlier!"

"I would have told you…"

"Would you, sir?" His father sighed. "Yes, I am sure you would. After a fashion. After the fashion of your telling me about your interview at the Royal Academy…"

Branwell turned away, moved across to the table, picked up one of the English soldiers. He said: "I believe there was a prejudice against me, sir. I fear that, being Londoners, they look down on Northerners at the Royal Academy. The sons of…"

"Parsons? Well, yes, perhaps they do."

"I meant sons of *Northerners*, sir. I did not seek to blame you, nor other parsons, beyond the general…"

"But perhaps it is true in some areas. Perhaps the Bradford patrons of your artist's workshop did not warm to the paintings of a parson's son. They, after all, have little reason to rail at Northerners. No, sir. Their geography, I think, would argue against it."

Branwell picked up the English soldier and also one of the French. He held them face to face. "I cannot deny my failure in the business of portraiture. Though many of my artistic friends – Mr Leyland the sculptor and his brother Francis for example – have often described my work in the most generous terms, frequently invoking the name of Mr Gainsborough." He began to manipulate the soldiers so they appeared to spar, then he dropped

26

them back on the table. He said: "The world of art is difficult, sir, at the best of times. There are fashions, modes, styles that must be caught at the instant, to make one appear attractive to the *hoi polloi*. If one is inclined to finer things, the matter of a Renaissance sensibility, certain eternal truths, then..."

Again his father interrupted. "Eternal truths, sir? What about catching the likeness of a sitter? Surely that is the main truth required in portraiture? Or am I become old-fangled, sir? Well, what exactly would you categorise as eternal truths?"

Branwell faced his father again. "Surely, sir, the brotherhood of mankind in which we honour and accept each other in every degree and kind and appetite..."

"That sounds to me, sir, like chapel talk, the rants of the radicals, the erstwhile revolutionaries of France..."

"Was not Wordsworth himself a supporter of that revolution? *Oh what a joy to be alive but to be young was very heaven!*"

"Heaven, sir, does not reside across the English Channel!"

"No, sir." Branwell averted his eyes.

"No, sir." His father also became subdued. "But I do accept your point that many of our greatest artists have suffered to be ignored much of their lives. It may still turn out, sir, that you are one of these." He looked at the letter again. "But you are not, it seems, one of our greatest *accountants!*"

"No, sir."

"No, sir! How could you have permitted this to happen, this loss of revenue revealed by the auditors? Surely the post of ticket clerk is not so arduous..."

"No indeed."

"Nor so irksome..."

"The clerking of tickets on the railway is an honourable post, father, and has many satisfactions. I was often praised during my employment for the elegance of my handwriting and the neatness of my style..."

Patrick jumped to his feet. "Pish! Your artistic friends again! You could *write* a ledger, it seems, at least enough so you caught the likeness. But could not *read* one adequately."

"No, sir." Branwell turned back to the table and began to draw circles with his fingers on the cloth. "It was during that period when I was most prodigious in my poetic output, Father, and perhaps my attention wandered from mundane matters. I remember now. I was translating Horace from the Latin."

A snort from his father. "Perhaps *Horace* is therefore to blame. But it is *we* will rue the day!"

Branwell raised an arm. He began: "*To Sestius.*
Rough winter melts beneath the breeze of spring.
Refitted ships shun not the silent sea,
Nor man nor beasts to folds or firesides cling,
Nor hoar frosts whiten over field and tree."

Patrick walked slowly across to Branwell and embraced him. "Oh!" he said, "my brilliant son!" There was a sudden catch in his throat.

Branwell allowed himself a smile. He said: "Thank you, father. I thought it caught the original…"

"…likeness. Yes, I believe it did."

"…yet newly fashioned in a selection of language properly used by modern man. As Mr Wordsworth says all modern poetry should be!" He pulled away from his father's grip. "I will find a new post, Father. I have made a good friend among the railway folk. There is one called Jacob who will…"

Suddenly his father was angry again. "*Railway folk!* Enough! No more clerking, sir, no more railways!" He still had the letter in his hand and he threw it on the floor. "A teaching post. That is what we must seek. It may well be you can inspire others. As I believe your sisters will. They are all bent on being governesses. Yes, yes. It is the only way forward."

"Yes," said Branwell, "teaching. You are right, Father. It is an honourable profession and has many satisfactions."

"It is agreed then."

"It is agreed, father."

In Branwell's head was music. And the words of Mr Bunyan.
He who would valiant be
Gainst all disaster
Let him in constancy

28

Follow the master.
There's no discouragement
Shall make him once relent
His first avowed intent
To be a pilgrim.

THERE WAS birdsong but Patrick was not aware of it. He had a mission. He had put on his black top hat and carried his ferruled black walking stick. He allowed himself one reassuring look back at the house, the workmanlike stone edifice, its walls the colour of the gravestones that fronted it. Then he moved on.

Brown lay on the grassy embankment smoking his clay pipe. He wore his cap against the sun and his workmen's overalls.

"Brown," said Patrick.

Brown took his pipe from his mouth. He did not look up. "Parson," he said.

"Are there no more graves to be dug?"

Still Brown did not look up. "Even a man of my calling must take his rest, Parson."

"I believe you are often here at this time of day."

"When fate allows." Brown looked skyward. "When the Great Geometer permits me."

"And I believe on occasion you encounter my son."

"Young Mr Branwell enjoys his daily ambulation, it is true. Ay, on occasion..."

"...you meet. And present him with a package."

"At his request. Always at *his* request."

"No more!"

Brown sniggered. "No more? Can any man say that to a gravedigger? Not even a parson."

Patrick was angry now. He clutched tightly the handle of his stick. "You forget yourself, sir!"

Brown stood up slowly, stretching out his legs and arms, loosening up. Then he looked at Patrick. Their eyes were level now. "Sir, I mean no offence. Young Mr Branwell considers me his friend." He emptied the pipe by knocking it against his leg then put it in his back pocket. "Sir, why do you pursue him so? Is

29

it not enough that he is part of this world, this great symmetry? Why not permit him his small radius, his tangent, his complementary angle?

"I do not consider you his friend."

"I am sorry for that, sir." Brown adjusted his cap. "For I consider myself a friend to everyone, all the inhabitants of this great sphere, this world of ours."

"This world of *yours*. Not mine, nor my son's." Patrick raised his stick slightly. "I know you, Brown."

"And I know you, sir. And I know your son."

"My son who can scarce dress himself by the middle of the day."

Brown smiled. "I will dress him, sir. I will be his manservant."

Now Patrick raised his stick above his head. Brown continued to smile. Patrick hesitated, lowered the stick, turned his back and walked away. He said as he went: "I know you, sir! I know you! Do not doubt that I do!"

Brown sat down on the grass again. He cupped his hand to his ear. "What?" he said. "I do not hear thee. I hear nowt. Speak up now, Parson! What, sir? What? *I do not hear thee!*"

BRANWELL STIRRED, looked about, found himself. He had been slumped over the desk. He had had a bad dream. He rubbed his eyes. "What?" he said, "What, sir? What? I do not hear you! I do not hear you!" What had the dream been about? He thought: *But is not all of this a dream then?* But no, it was not.

"I must write! My novel! Where is my novel? I must work." He searched the drawers, found the dog-eared sheets. "Here! Ah, yes! Yes!" He spread them out on the desk top. Surely there were more pages? Surely there were other sheets? Well, well, he had found these; he would find the rest. Eventually. He had *not* lost his novel. No. He had not lost his work.

He read, perhaps in his head, perhaps aloud: "Book One, Chapter 17. *In the House.*" He cleared his throat. *That* was not in his head. "He made no halt in his intrusion on the quietude of the Hall. He was received by the Lady of the Mansion in the breakfast room..." *Breakfast room*? The library, perhaps, was more elegant. No, no. Breakfast was more *intimate*. "No servant could have been so dull as not to perceive the change in their calm and sweet-tempered mistress. The dove-like eye now seemed troubled; the voice with its gentle tone, now gave way to hesitation…" *Gave way* to hesitation? *Harboured* hesitation? No. No. *Gave way*. He thought: *Yes, This is good. It stands the test of time.* "She recalled the promise lately given to her furious husband, but a still small voice told the lady that her visitor had feelings of a wider, higher and deeper range than her…" Her *husband?* No, that was repetition. Her *spouse*? Spouse, then! Still, small, voice. Yes, *spouse* was more alliterative with those adjacent words. He made the alteration. Lady? Wife? No, no! Lady! Told the *lady*. There. Keep it. The *l* and the *d* were most evocative. There!

He sat back in his chair. He suddenly wished for something of a contrast. He reached for the decanter but stopped himself. Where… ? He shuffled the sheets. He opened the drawer once more and felt about blindly until…Yes. He had found some more.

He pulled out the sheets. He read: "Book Two, Chapter Three. *In the Garden*." He coughed. "It was late August and the sun was still warm. He turned the corner by the daffodils and came once more upon the lady…" *Daffodils?* Chrysanthemums perhaps. Chrysanthemums were more in accord with the seasons. "But," he thought, "I am not so much a naturalist as I am a novelist. And the daffodils might well be nigh spent. Yes, yes, it is therefore a more telling image." He read: "She turned, affrighted, at the sound of his footfall and leaned against the tall ash tree." Ash? Oak? *Oak* was more masculine but perhaps too much for one so genteel. *Ash* then. Leave it.

He put down the novel, again reached out for the decanter, again thought better of it. He said: "Well, there it is, Mr Editor. Soon it shall wend its way towards your publishing house. If only life were as elegant and as wholesome as my novel, Mr Editor, as the novels which fall – plop! – on your desk every day. But in life… In *my* life…"

He picked up another sheet. It was a letter to Leyland which he should have posted. He read: "Leyland, my old friend, sculptor and scholar, teacher of my art… I have to tell you there is a lady about whom I have high hopes though much concealed. She has been until recently a married woman, but this state is no more. Her husband, my erstwhile employer, has lately shaken off this mortal coil, as Mr Shakespeare says. I therefore wait each day, breathless, to hear from her. I wait..." He sighed. "But she is surrounded by powerful persons who hate me. The husband has left his property in trust to the widow provided I do not see her. If I disobey, it is to ruin her. But I dare hope she will take courage..." He took his eyes from the letter. Oh, he knew *this* one by heart.

"Though I write about a love concealed, I tell you truly no servant could have been so dull as not to perceive the change in their calm and sweet-tempered mistress. The dove-like eye seemed troubled; the voice with its gentle tone gave way to hesitation..." Yes, it was no longer merely a voice in his head. "To tear from my heart the thousand recollections of her that rush upon me would be to steal from a newly blind man his remembrance of sunlight." He stopped. "Yes. Yes. That's good."

He dropped the letter on the desk top and walked across to the table. He picked up two soldiers, both English, both in the blood-red uniform. He said: "Leyland, old friend, it would be disheartening to work myself up again to new battles. I have already been compelled to retreat with heavy loss and no gain. My army stands now where it did then, and I mourn the slaughter of my youth and hope." He carried the soldiers back to his desk. Oh, it was good that he had not yet posted the letter. He would add to it. He sat down and again picked up the quill. He wrote: "While I am thus writing, old friend and tutor, may I also mention my embarrassment with an outstanding bill at The Old Cock in Halifax. It is a mere three shillings, but I have been threatened with a court summons. You yourself are a valued customer. I wonder if you might reassure the landlady of my reliability in such matters? Your good and faithful friend as ever, P.B. Bronte."

He dropped the letter on the desk, picked up another sheet at random. He studied it for a moment then read: "Oh, Lydia, my love, mistress of my heart, I have to tell you that you are a lady about whom I have high hopes though much concealed. You have been until recently a married woman, but this state is no more. I do hope your husband, now he is freed from the dungeon of this life, as was Christian in Mr Bunyan's tale, will receive in heaven that honour and respect for every degree, kind and appetite which is sadly absent here on earth. Meanwhile I wait each day, breathless, to hear from you. You are surrounded by powerful persons who hate me. Yet I dare hope you will take courage and reveal your true self to me. Though our love has long been a love concealed on both our parts, yet no servant could have been so dull as not to perceive the change in your calm and sweet-tempered demeanour. To tear from my heart the thousand recollections of you would be to steal from a newly blind man his remembrance of sunlight." Yes, it was *very* good. "Also," he added, "I have written a poem, which I enclose." But where was it? He still had a version somewhere. He had already sent it out, but he would not have risked his original. He stood up, opened first one drawer then another. Ah. Here. Here after all.

He read:
"I see your picture is cleverly made.
Where should be sunshine, there is shade.
And from your heart your smiles still shine
Though you have stolen all from mine."

Ah yes. He pressed it to the front of his dressing gown. He went back to the letter. He wrote: "And I have sent a copy already to the *Bradford Herald*. I await their letter of acceptance. Your stout-hearted servant, PB Bronte."

Then he sat down again at the desk, reached out for the decanter, filled his glass and emptied it at a single gulp. And he was suddenly aware of a woman sobbing. *Another* dream? No. There was someone else in the room...

SHE WAS sitting there at the table, one hand against the side of her head. How could he not have been aware of her? He got to his feet and ran across.

"Charlotte!" he cried, "Sister! What is it?" He was alarmed now. "Oh my poor Mary Percy! Let Zamorna comfort you!"

Charlotte pulled away from him. "I do not need the comfort of Zamorna! I do not need the comfort of a toy soldier!"

"Sister, do not reject me! Do not leave me in my misery."

At this she turned to him, showing her drawn and tear-stained face. "*Your* misery! *Branwell's* misery! What misery is that? The misery of the table-top? The blood and tears of toyland? Or were those real battles we fought here? Was this wood once truly stained with the lifeblood of the infantry? Because I look, I look, and I cannot see the stains. Nor do I smell the smoke of cannon. I sniff the fuggy air and smell only the sourness of gin!"

"I have had a *glass*, sister! That is all. To help with my writing."

"I have not read your writing for many a year, brother. For now it is sealed away in an envelope and bears a new-fangled postage stamp. You write *letters*, Branwell!" She paused. "Not that you ever post them."

"No, no, I do not write *only* letters. You mistake me. I am a *man* of letters." He giggled. "I would not want you to think I write only letters. No. No. Poems. I write poems. At this very moment, I wait on acceptance from the local paper."

"Poems!" He could tell nothing from her tone. "And what is your subject?"

For a moment he considered not telling her. Then he blurted out: "My subject is love!"

"A noble subject." She made herself laugh. "Girls' games! Are not the games of love mere girls' games?"

He was wounded by her words. "*These* are no games! *I* do not play at love!"

"Do you not? Does someone then play with *you*?"

"I do not understand."

"I also do not understand. There is always love. Else what will the soldiers do when they have won? They must have something to do when the battle is over." She held up a crumpled sheet of paper in her hand. "*You* write *your* letters, brother, and *I* write *mine*! But I *post* mine! And now it is sent back to me. A rejection from the publisher of my heart!"

Branwell was suddenly afraid. Charlotte said: "I will show you. I will explain. It will not make pretty reading. It is not at all like Miss Austen."

By this time he was in full retreat, back to his desk, back to his papers, back to the high-backed chair. Charlotte followed him, dragging her own chair. They sat together. He did not like their faces to be suddenly so close.

"Look!" She pointed to the letter. "It is a long time since you have read what *I* write, brother. These are the kind of letters *I* write!"

He turned away. "If these are words of moment, sister, if these are words close to your heart and person, then I would feel an intruder to read them."

"If you will *not* read them, *I* will read them to you. Your subject is love. And so is mine."

"And to whom do you write of your love?"

"My professor."

"I do not..."

"...understand? You keep saying so, brother, yet I think you *do* understand. Else I would not bother with you. Now. Listen." She began to read. "I have done everything. I have sought occupation. I have denied myself absolutely the pleasure of speaking about you. But I have been able to conquer neither my regrets nor my impatience." She turned to Branwell. "Is this familiar to you, brother? Does this strike a chord with your emotions? With your poetic intellect?"

He struggled to make sense of her. "Your *professor*? You mean..."

"Monsieur Constantine. The constant one. The head of my school. Where I worked and taught. And learned."

Branwell was horror-struck. The *monsieur*! The Belgian! "You have formed an attachment with a Belgian?"

"The *monsieur*. Yes. We all called him that."

"But he is foreign. And a member of the Church of Rome!"

"I have heard that Byron died a Catholic. Though you would not notice from his verses."

Branwell put a hand to his brow. "Sister, do not continue. It is unseemly that you divulge this..."

"...passion?"

"...*liaison*."

"Oh. And I thought you did not know your French. Strange how the English always find a French word to describe the very thing of which they disapprove. But your new poem... Is that in English?"

"Of course it is in English."

"And the whole world may read it? Whichever part of the world buys the *Halifax Guardian*?"

"It is the *Bradford Herald*!" It was *his* turn to be angry.

"*Touché!*" The laughter was genuine this time. "There. Another French word for your vocabulary. My own French is *tres pauvre*, I'm afraid. When I write in French, the *monsieur* corrects my sentences. Sometimes also when I write in English."

He saw of a sudden a chance to comfort her. "Believe me – your English sentences are excellent."

She looked hard at him. "Thank you," she said.

He had now seen his chance to change the subject. "But in my case we speak of a poem. We speak of rhyme and metre..."

"Assonance and alliteration, no doubt."

"Perhaps. Though at this moment I forget some details of the style..."

"But *not* the content! You do not forget the *content*!" She was almost shouting now. She sounded a little like Father.

"I do *not* forget the content." His own voice was quieter.

"The *hurt*! We none of us forget the hurt!"

He floundered. "This thing of yours is not a poem. This is..."

"A letter. Naked. For a letter does not wear the garments of rhyme and metre."

"And you are not a poet! You are a woman! And women..."

"... must not talk of such things. Women must not show themselves naked. Not even in words. But you have seen *me* naked, brother. Is that not so?"

"When we were children. We are not children now."

"Are we not? I can never make up my mind about that. But yes, you are right. A letter is always naked if it is sincere. It can never pretend to be a poem. But listen how it speaks to you."

She started to read again. "It is indeed humiliating to be unable to control one's thoughts, to be the slave of regret, of memory, the slave of a fixed and dominant idea which lords it over the mind. Your last letter was a stay and prop to me, nourishment for half a year..."

"Stop!" said Branwell, "This is unseemly."

Her voice was growing now with the emotion. "To forbid me to write to you, to refuse to answer me, would be to tear from me my only joy on earth, to deprive me of my final privilege. Believe me, my master, so long as I believe you are pleased with me, so long as I have hope of receiving news from you, I can be at rest and not too sad. But when day by day I await a letter and when day by day disappointment flings me back in overwhelming sorrow, then fever claims me..."

"Stop!" He was frantic now.

" ...I lose appetite and sleep. I pine away."

"Stop!"

Now she stopped. Now she held the letter high above her head. "He sent it back. He sent it back unopened." She crumpled it and threw it across the room.

Branwell said: "Perhaps his wife..."

"Of *course* his wife! But is he not a *man*? Does he not have the courage...?"

Branwell now saw his opportunity. "It is well that he sends it back. He has done right by you. I am your brother. And a poet. And I can see that words which may flow in perfect innocence from a young lady like yourself might with others be taken amiss."

"How?"

"They might be thought to mean more than they do. They might be thought to take on a carnal aspect."

For a moment she looked on him unbelieving. "A *carnal aspect*? Is this how modern poets write of love?" And then she said: "And if that carnal aspect were true?"

Branwell leapt to his feet. "Charlotte, you besmirch yourself to talk like this!"

Charlotte also stood. "Because I am not a *man*? Because a woman must never confess to a carnal aspect?"

37

"You are not yourself. That is the fact of the matter. You have been upset..."

"*Deeply* upset."

"*Deeply* upset. By this letter. But sanity will return."

"To which of us, brother? To which of us will sanity return? I think sometimes pain has its own intelligence, that it seeks out those who are weak in this or that way and devises a narrow strategy for each of us. *To be rejected*! That was always the worst fear for me. And my pain, my very clever pain, knows this. But I have cast it down, this pain, this sorrow, I have crumpled it and cast it on the floor and I will walk across the room and step on it."

She walked across the room and did so. She said: "Of *course* it's his wife!"

Words came unbidden into Branwell's head. He found himself saying: "My Lydia is not like that."

Charlotte looked across at him in surprise.

Now he had started, he found he could not stop. "My Lydia knows my pain and comforts me. But there are others. There are those who hate me. They surround her. They whisper about me. Now her husband is dead. And I am sorry for it. For I wish no man harm. Yet I see the hand of God in it all."

A look of amazement crossed Charlotte's face. "The hand of God? Lydia?" And suddenly it dawned. "Your *employer's wife*!" She leaned against the table. "How alike we are, you and I. We go out into the world and we take our madness with us."

"It is *not* madness!"

"What a vile, corrupt breed we teachers are! All of us who think we have something to give the world. We give only our insanity. How often does she write?"

"I tell you. There are those close to her who hate me. It is difficult for her to write."

"Difficult! What is there in life that is not *difficult*?" She walked back to him and cradled his head on her breast. She said: "We are still friends, it seems. Good. I thought for a while we were not."

He hugged her like a toddler hugging its mother. "We will always be friends. We are alike."

"Even though you are a boy and boys have larger brains?"

"Even so."

"Well, I suppose you are right. We have no secrets. We have seen each other naked. When we were children. And are we not still children now?"

THERE WAS a wind-up tin music box playing *God Rest Ye Merry, Gentlemen*, but it gave up and ran down after the first chorus. Patrick said: "It is good to have my family about me. Christmas is a time for families."

They were sitting round the table in the study with a bottle of Bordeaux for father and a jug of orange juice for themselves.

Charlotte said: "I am sure Branwell will be back shortly, father."

Emily said: "There is, I believe, some revelry in the village. The Christmas Eve sort that involves the men."

Anne said: "You mean involves strong drink."

Charlotte said: "But I am sure he will be back tonight."

Emily said: "Or early tomorrow. In time for his presents, no doubt. I am giving him my old copy of *A Christmas Carol*. To remind him what Christmas is about."

"I know the one you mean. The spine is torn and you have pencilled many comments in the margins. That is not much of a Christmas present, Emily. He will think you are a veritable Jacob Marley." This from Anne.

"Let him think rather I am the Spirit of Christmas Yet to Come. That might do him some good."

"Oh come now," said Patrick, "Branwell is a young man. And young men..."

"No, no. He is not so young," Emily interrupted. "He merely affects to be young. He still keeps toy soldiers in his drawer"

"You are harsh with him at times," Patrick took a sip of his wine.

"No more than he deserves," said Emily, "No more than you, father."

And Patrick said: "I am tired. I will retire to bed." He drained his glass. "I am grown old. Once I could control his ways. Once I could control *your* ways, daughters. Now I must let you come and go as you please. But Branwell is still my son." To emphasise his words, he put down his glass and knocked against the corner of the table.

INSIDE THE old cottage at the end of the cobbled High Street, for ten years used by the Masons, John Brown gave three loud knocks on the door of the Room of Ceremonies and both men entered. It was empty. The three knocks had been symbolic, Branwell knew, perhaps representing the Trinity. Or the Three wise Men. He was not sure.

John Brown wore a black robe that resembled the gown of a barrister. Branwell wore a white robe and a white silk blindfold.

John Brown said: "Welcome, my son. Welcome, my brother. Welcome."

Branwell put his hands together in the sign of prayer. "Thanks to you, father. Thanks to you, brother."

"Today is the day, my son, my brother, to receive from thy holy father and true brother the rites of initiation. Does tha wish that? Does tha wish to join us in the true knowledge?"

"With all my heart."

"Tha's been divested already of what monies tha carried, so tha comes to this temple bereft of the help and support of this world."

"I have. I do."

"Then let the ritual begin. Thee is a poor candidate in a state of darkness..."

"I am."

"And tha comes of thy own free will and accord, humbly soliciting to be admitted to the mysteries and privileges of Freemasonry..."

"I do."

"Kneel."

Branwell knelt. He knew, for they had rehearsed this often of late, that on the table lay a large leather-bound book, a silver plated jug filled with wine, two silver plated tankards, and a short sword in imitation of the Roman legions. He felt the sword touch his left shoulder, then his right; his right shoulder then his left. He heard the clatter as the sword was returned to the table. He knew that John Brown had now picked up the book.

John Brown began to read. His tone was solemn as befitted a marriage. He said: "Tha must know that all men are a measure of the world..."

"I know."

"It is their only value and significance."

"So I have learned."

"They reflect the perfect proportions of the Great Geometer..."

ANNE SAID: "I wish he would see the error of his ways. But he has no sense of proportion."

"Come, daughter. It is the season of good will."

And Charlotte said sharply: "We do not wish to worry our father unduly."

"You are all young women of great virtue. Sometimes it is hard for a young woman to understand the nature of a man. But I, though I am old and somewhat damaged by the world, I do understand Branwell, I *do*."

"It is a phase," said Charlotte, "It will pass. It is like a wild passage in a concerto by Vivaldi. It will be replaced by a slower movement. That is the nature of music. The fast and the slow. It will calm him."

"But," said Emily, "Branwell only listens to the music in his head."

"Then, sister, he is not the only one in this family who does so. Not the only one who *dances* to it."

"If you mean me, Charlotte..."

"I do."

"Dancer, indeed! I did not think to cut such a dashing figure!"

"ALL MEN," said John Brown, "are mere figures and fractions. Is not an inch the length of thy fingernail?"

"It is."

"And twelve the length of thy foot?"

"Yes, yes."

"And a yard is the measure of thine arm and thy leg and thy reach and thy stride?"

"Yes."

"Is not a stone that weighs a pound the natural limit of thy grasp and lift? Why does tha seek to lift more?"

"I do not."

"But once tha did. Once tha sought to move mountains."

"No longer."

"Tha's become a sounding brass and a tinkling cymbal."

"I renounce those ways."

"And what is now thine ambition?"

"To be as all my brothers, my fellow men. To be no more than the lowest."

"I rejoice to hear it."

"I also rejoice."

"WE SHOULD rejoice!" said Patrick, "We should not have such long faces. We should rejoice in our saviour who has put us on this earth to do good works."

Anne was suddenly alert. "*Good works*! Why, yes, our good works should be celebrated. Father..."

But Charlotte interrupted. "It is never right that we should boast of our good works, sister. Such an action brings demerit upon them and upon ourselves." And then to Emily: "Does it not, sister?"

"Charlotte is right. Whited sepulchres are never pleasing to the Lord."

"But sometimes," said Anne, "when the news is good, is it not our duty to communicate it? Would it not raise people's spirits if it were known?"

"And others might be condemned to purgatory. Better sometimes to keep our secrets, sister. At least till time is ripe." Charlotte put a finger to her lips.

Patrick looked from one to the other. "Secrets? You bemuse me with your talk. What secrets can young women of virtue ever have? You jest with an old man." And he laughed. The first time time that night, thought Charlotte.

"THIS IS the secret," said John Brown, "which we now share with thee. For we are entering a new age when all numbers shall be levelled and all shall be as one!" He removed Branwell's blindfold. "Now for the first time tha can truly see. Look around thee, lad. Gaze upon thy new world."

Branwell looked about the room, the oil lamps, the drawn curtains. "The world is beautiful," he said.

"But do not seek to be more than tha can be. Be humble. Any help and support tha may receive can only come now as a gift from thy fellow Masons. Here, let us now take God's gift of wine by which thy new life may be consecrated."

And Branwell suddenly realised how much of a thirst he had.

CHARLOTTE AND Anne were seated at the table with the half-empty wine bottle, the jug with its dregs of orange and the empty glasses. Emily stood by the desk, holding a book in a brown paper cover with the label PRINTER'S PROOF. She read: "This is certainly a beautiful country! In all England I do not believe I could have fixed on a situation so completely removed from the stir of society."

"Well done," cried Anne, "Well done, Mr Bell! Well done, *Wuthering Heights*! I see from the very start of your novel that you draw strongly upon your own life and situation, sir."

Charlotte said: "You could not be more removed, sir, from the stir of society than to be here with your sisters..."

"Brothers!" Anne interrupted.

Charlotte corrected herself. "Brothers! Brother writers! The Bells!" She pointed to Emily. "Ellis Bell!" Then to Anne. "Acton Bell!" Then to herself. " Currer Bell!"

"The Bells of the Ball!" said Anne and they all laughed.

"Come, Emily," said Charlotte, "be not so shy. Let us have more."

Emily smiled. Was it shyness or a wilful coyness? "Which passage do you request?"

Charlotte considered. "Why, it should be something involving that eccentric Mr Heathcliff! Do you not think so, Anne? For he has fast become my favourite character in all English fiction."

"Your favourite *male* character, you mean!" This from Anne.

"Let me see," said Emily. She turned the pages. "Well, I shall risk this one, if it please you. Though it is hardly festive reading." She took a deep breath and began: " 'I shall join you directly,' said Heathcliff, 'Keep out of the yard, though. The dogs are unchained.' I obeyed, as far as to quit the chamber; when I was witness, involuntarily, to a piece of superstition which belied oddly Mr Heathcliff's apparent sense. He got onto the bed and wrenched open the lattice, bursting as he pulled at it into an uncontrollable passion of tears. 'Come in, come in!' he sobbed, 'Cathy, do come! Oh do – once more! Oh my heart's darling! Hear me this time!' The spectre gave no sign of being, but the snow and wind whirled wildly through, blowing out the light."

"Ghosts," said Anne, "are ever a part of Christmas, are they not? Oh, it makes me shiver!"

"It makes us *all* shiver!" agreed Charlotte. Then to Emily: "But do I not see in the character of your Mr Heathcliff a reflection of your own demeanour, Mr Bell?"

"He is always brooding," said Anne, "like yourself, Mr Bell. He has that air of Lord Byron..."

"Is it not a self-portrait, Mr Bell?" asked Charlotte, "Will it not perhaps become a bad influence on the younger generation of women? Will it not set the minds of young girls a-racing?"

"Their hearts a-fluttering!" said Anne.

"Their hair streaming back in the wind as they run across the heather-strewn moors?" suggested Charlotte.

"Dreaming of their *own* Mr Heathcliff?" from Anne.

They collapsed in laughter once again – a trifle theatrically, thought Emily.

Charlotte said: "Well, sir, and what do you say to us?"

"I do not write for young girls, sir. If they should succumb to such bestial charms..."

"*Bestial charms*!" said Anne, "Why, that is a phrase to be savoured, Mr Bell."

Charlotte said: "Then for whom do you write?"

"I write for myself, Mr Bell..."

"How selfish of you, Mr Bell!" Charlotte looked quite stern. "But sometimes perhaps we *must* be selfish. We *must* do things for ourselves."

"We?"

Anne said: "Women. Do you mean women, Mr Bell?"

Charlotte clapped her hands. "What do I know of women, Mr Bell? I who am a bachelor?" She turned to Anne. "Come, Mr Bell, let us hear from your own celebrated work. Let us hear from Agnes Grey."

Emily and Anne exchanged places. Now Anne was the reader and she too had her PRINTER'S PROOF.

Emily said: "Read me the part where she decides to leave home. I like that."

Anne thumbed through the book, found the place and started reading: " 'I should like to be a governess,' I said. My mother uttered an exclamation of surprise, and laughed. My sister dropped her work in astonishment, exclaiming: 'You a governess, Agnes! What can you be dreaming of?' "

Charlotte said: "I am amazed, Mr Bell. How can you dream so wantonly as to place yourself in the mind of a young girl? And, even more astonishing, one who wishes to be a governess! It is so far removed from your actual existence that I marvel at your powers of imagination!"

"She must certainly suffer for her ambition," said Emily, "Do you not think so, Mr Bell? Read us now a passage where she suffers terribly! Read me the scene where she is tormented by that abominable snob Miss Murray."

"Wait, wait! Yes, I have it!" Anne read: " 'Miss Grey,' said Miss Murray, as I was perusing a long and extremely interesting letter of my sister's, 'Do put away that dull, stupid letter, and listen to me! You should tell the good people at home not to bore you with such long letters.' 'The good people at home,' replied I, 'know very well that the longer their letters are, the better I like them.' 'Well,' said Miss Murray, 'I want to talk about the ball; and to tell you that you positively must put off your holidays till it is over.' 'But,' I said, 'I cannot disappoint my friends by postponing my return so long. I cannot bear the thoughts of a Christmas spent from home.' "

Emily liked that. "I like it that your Agnes should stand up for herself, stand up against the world. Stand up against the likes of Miss Murray."

But Charlotte was suddenly melancholy. "Well, Christmas at home. That is a subtle victory and a mixed blessing perhaps. But it is something a governess will understand."

Anne said: "Was not your own book about a governess?"

Charlotte looked away. "It was. And you will recall it was rejected by your publisher, despite the promise of payment from the author. Unlike your own works, which are now about to enjoy great celebrity..."

"Nobody will read them," said Emily, "We have paid towards their publication and yet..."

"...we cannot pay the readers to read them. We had only *one* legacy from our poor Aunt." Anne returned to the table, to the remaining chair.

"But," said Charlotte, "at least they will be out in the world. At least they do not fester at home, as we do. At Christmas time or any other. Do you regret it then? Would you rather have spent the money on petticoats and bracelets?"

Anne reacted immediately. "No, sister! I rejoice in being an authoress. And it is you who are the organiser of that."

"No, no," said Charlotte, "An *author*, Mr Bell. You are authors and you are men!" She turned to Emily. "And you, Mr Bell?"

Emily thought about it. "To me it makes no difference, Mr Bell. And yet... Perhaps it *was* good that we should do it. Even though I know not why."

Anne turned to Charlotte. "But you, Mr Bell, you are the one who provoked us to this action. It is unfair that you yourself should remain unpublished."

"The world is never fair, Mr Bell. Come, let us drink the health of your publisher. God bless the man and rest him merry!"

They finished what was left of the orange juice.

Anne said: "Surely you have not surrendered your own literary hopes, Mr Bell?"

"No, no," said Charlotte, "I am now working on a new tale. And I will seek out a new publisher. It is about a plain girl and I have called her Jane. I fear she is somewhat like myself."

"Is she a governess?" asked Emily.

"I have not truly made up my mind on that score yet."

"She *will* be a governess, I know it!" said Emily.

Anne added: "When you are published also, then we shall tell Father. You will surely allow that?"

"But how," said Emily, "shall we ever tell Branwell? Tell me, Mr Bell. Tell me, Mr Organiser."

Charlotte sighed. "If we are truly to be the Bells of the Ball, then we must learn to enjoy our secrets, smile behind our paper fans as we gaze at the dancing crowd. Let us keep our own counsel on the matter. At least for now. But it is good to talk like this. I am glad Father has gone to bed."

There was a sudden banging on the back door. And Branwell's voice. A *drunken* Branwell. "Hey there! Let us in!"

And another voice: "We demand admission!"

"It is John Brown," said Emily.

And Branwell again: "Unless you be in a state of undress!"

"Even that I by no means deplore!" shouted Brown. And there was the sound of raucous male laughter.

"We are *not* in a state of undress!" shouted Emily.

"Heaven forbid!" said Anne more quietly.

Charlotte got to her feet. "We had best let them in then! We cannot afford them waking Father. But remember – keep our own counsel."

The others nodded. Emily went to the door. Branwell and Brown came in, jaunty, self-satisfied, staggering slightly. Branwell removed his hat – a grey topper that had seen better days. He smiled in an exaggerated way. He said: "Forgive us, ladies, for disturbing you!"

"Why," asked Charlotte, "do men always believe they are disturbing to women? And yet apologise for it?"

Brown said: "Thee is right, Miss Charlotte. There are too many apologies in this world. Let us be simply as we are, with no apologies. I for one pledge never to apologise." He took off his own hat, a blue workman's cap which he waved as he made a clumsy bow.

"But we are sinners, Mr Brown. And we must sometimes apologise to God." This from Anne.

"I have brought John home with me..." said Branwell.

Emily was studying Brown with interest, Charlotte noticed. Emily said: "I can *see* you have brought Mr Brown home with you."

"Or *he* has brought *you* home." From Anne.

"I can see you have been drinking. You have both been drinking." From Charlotte.

"No apologies, Miss Charlotte," said Brown. He wandered across to the table, put his cap on it and suddenly lifted his hand with something red poking out from his fingers. "I have a rifleman here!"

Charlotte said: "It is General Percy. We have failed to tidy him away."

Branwell said: "No apologies, sister."

Brown said: "It has been a good night. Good for..."

"Conversation," said Branwell,

"Argument," said Brown.

"Philosophy."

"We have seen eternity tonight."

"*Like a great ring of pure and endless light/ All calm as it was bright...*"

"Three hundred and sixty degrees as described by Euclid..."

"I do not think that our brother was talking mathematics, Mr Brown..."

"Was he not, Miss Anne?"

"Was I not?" Branwell sounded confused.

"For what is philosophy, Miss Anne, except mathematics? What is the universe except an equation? A proof?"

"A proof of what?"

"Of itself, Miss Charlotte."

"There," said Anne, "we must differ, Mr Brown. To me and to my family, the universe is a manifestation of the love of God, a proof of that love."

Brown looked at her and his face screwed up into a mask of exaggerated pity. "And what love has he shown to thee, Miss Anne, who has lost a mother and two sisters?" Then to the room he said: "Well, what is love? As a tennis score it is nothing.

Nowt. And on to that first nothing we can add a string of nothings and make hundreds and thousands and millions. Just by adding nowt and nowt and nowt."

Anne said: "You are playing parlour games, Mr Brown."

"But let him," said Emily, "I find it amusing."

"Yes," said Branwell. He began to peer about him and adjusted his spectacles, "Amusing."

"What is eternity then, if not mathematics, ladies? What is infinity? Well, I will tell thee: there is more than one infinity, as there is more than one God."

"That is blasphemy, Mr Brown."

"Mere truth, Miss Charlotte. For tha must allow there be an infinite number of numbers in the world. For numbers, like God, have no end."

"I do."

"But numbers are divided into odds and evens. And the number of even numbers is also infinite."

"Well..."

"And for that matter, the number of odd numbers is infinite too."

"Ah, I see it," said Emily.

"I too see it!" said Branwell, "Indeed I do!"

"So we have already identified three separate infinities, have we not? And we have hardly begun. So many infinities!"

"'So many *gods*!" said Branwell.

"*Branwell!*"

"I do not mean..." began Branwell.

"I think he was using metaphor, Miss Charlotte. I know from experience Mr Branwell is a master of metaphor. But it sometimes runs away with him."

"If there are many infinities, then there are many truths..."

"Yes! Oh, tha's such a bright one, Miss Emily! All those truths! But not in the sense that *parish records* are a truth. *What-does-tha-call-him was born on such-and-such and died on so-and-so.*" Brown put his hand on his heart. "*And I do attach to this document my signature that it is a true and accurate record.* For when people die, then there is a need of a parish record kind of truth. But epitaphs – are they also truths? *Gone to his Maker?*

Do we know that for a parish record kind of truth? I think we do not. *Loved by all*? Show me a man who is loved by all and I'll eat a sod from the graveyard! No, no, not parish record truth at all! And all those *poems*. And all those *novels*..."

"What truth are they, Mr Brown? For I have ambitions in that area."

"Does tha now, Miss Emily? Why, it is any truth tha could want! For a writer is like God, is he not? He makes a Universe on the page and sometimes we say: *yes, it is true, it speaks to me of the world.* But we know it is not the parish record kind of true. We know we cannot put our signatures to it and say: *this is an accurate record.* Suppose, for instance, in a century's time, some writer might make a little story out of all of us..."

Emily giggled. "Why should he do that?"

"Who knows? *I* am not a writer. Perhaps he has taken against us. Taken against *me*. He might make me out the Devil Incarnate if he wanted. He might write anything he liked. And it might not bear one word of truth." Brown looked at the soldier in his hand. "Oh yes, he might treat us all like little toy soldiers, play with us, move us about, snap off our heads..." And he snapped off the soldier's head and threw the soldier across the room.

Emily put a hand to her mouth. She said: "Was that not General Percy?"

Branwell fell to his knees, picked up the body with his right hand and the head with his left. He said: "We can perhaps repair him."

John Brown strode across to Emily. He stared at her. "But thee, Miss Emily... Oh yes, I should like to read a novel written by thee. I should not be surprised if thee did not turn out the brightest star in the vault!" Then he looked away, embarrassed. "That is to say, the vault of *heaven* of course. Though I am a gravedigger, yet I did not mean anything so unfeeling as the *family* vault. No offence intended!"

"None taken!" said Branwell.

"None at all!" said Emily.

"So numbers govern everything, Mr Brown? Not love, nor decency, nor sense of duty? Only numbers."

"Does not the Bible itself tell us this, Miss Charlotte? *For I saw a new heaven and a new earth! And at the Gates twelve angels! And on the gates the names of the twelve tribes of Israel! And the wall of the city had twelve foundations and on them the twelve names of the twelve apostles!* And are there not twelve pence in a shilling? And will that state not continue evermore till the very crack of doom?"

Branwell gasped. "It must be so!"

"And are we not all here, ladies, to make up the ledger as the Great Accountant demands? And is that not enough?" He turned again to Emily. "It is a shame there is no music in this house tonight, for Mr Branwell and I have been discussing music."

"And if there were, Mr Brown, what should we do?"

"Why then, Miss Emily, we should dance!"

"It would wake Father!"

"Not if we dance without music. We can easily do so. All we need are the measures!" He stepped forward, took hold of her right hand, put his own right arm round her waist. "One-two-three, one-two-three, one-two-three! One-two-three, one-two-three, one-two-three! One-two-three, one-two-three, one-two-three!" Suddenly, somehow, they were waltzing, round and round, albeit comic and clumsy. They had made two complete circles of the room before Emily pulled away.

"No, no, Mr Brown! It is too strange!"

"Strange, Miss Emily? No, no, there is no strangeness." He had become still now, but remained awkward, graceless; he looked about the room. "We are all of a muchness, are we not? All of a mean and an average? So why do we strive, to be other than we are? Are we not already sufficient?"

"Yes," said Branwell, "It is so!"

Charlotte leapt to her feet. "No, Mr Brown! No, brother! We are not in this world to make up the numbers! We are here to show our Maker who and what we are! Yes, Mr Brown, we *are* here to strive!"

"But sister..."

"Hush, Branwell! We have heard enough of *you*!" Charlotte turned to address Emily. "And you, sister! I condemn you for your slatternly behaviour!"

"I do not understand..." Emily began.

"Look at this room! Is this what passes for neatness in your outlandish world? Is it tidy? Is it right? Is it fit for a Christian family? Must we not labour far more diligently to clear away the bric-a-brac?"

Charlotte picked up the besom from the recess in the wall. She said: "You dance, Mr Brown? You enjoy the dance? You admire the terpsichorean art?"

"Why, yes, Miss..."

Charlotte came at him with the broom, knocking it against his legs, banging his ankles, forcing him round the room, one circle, two circles. Brown was crying: "Miss Charlotte! Miss Charlotte!" And finally: "Miss Emily!"

And Emily laughed. And Anne was laughing too. And then Charlotte stopped and *she* began to laugh. "Yes, Mr Brown, we are here to strive! And now I would be happy if you were to strive to leave this house."

For a moment he was quiet, sullen. Then: "If that is thy wish, ma'am. If that is the wish of the other ladies. If that is the wish of Miss Emily..."

He walked across to the table and picked up his hat, then moved back towards Emily. He stared at her. She dropped her eyes. "Oh, for thee, bright Emily, for thee I would..."

Emily raised her glance. "What would you do, Mr Brown?"

"Why, I would hang a litter of puppies!" and he turned on his heel, with no sign of the loping drunkenness of earlier. He walked sharply to the back door, opened it and was gone.

Branwell turned on Charlotte. "You have insulted my friend!"

Charlotte ignored him. She said to the girls: "Come. It is late and there will be even more jollification in the morning. We must be ready for the high spirits of the day." She replaced the besom in the recess.

As the three of them trooped out towards the stairs, Charlotte took Emily's arm. "Plain Jane. She *will* be a governess. I know her well. I am good at governesses."

BRANWELL STOOD for a while. He was alone now. As it seemed he had always been. A piece of music ran through his head. It was *The Radetzky March* by Herr Strauss which he had heard played by an orchestra in Bradford only a few weeks previous. It was very military, of course. That would be why he was reminded of it tonight. The accident to General Percy. Most unfortunate. And yet it might perhaps be put right. But Charlotte had insulted his friend. She had... His friend was *lost*.

He walked across to the desk. He opened the drawers, pulled out the papers, threw them down as he did so. Occasionally he would proclaim. "The Editor of Blackwoods. Sir, Read what I write. It is right that you must. I trust you will not think me used and stale that I have already been published in the *Halifax Guardian*." He laughed.

"The Secretary, The Royal Academy. Sir, We had arranged an appointment but there was family business. That is plain truth. I swear it. My family inquired of Mr Turner and Mr Gainsborough. But these great artists would not permit me to call on you." Another laugh rose in his throat but did not escape his lips.

"The Directors of the Leeds and Manchester Railroad. I write to bring to your attention a very grave injustice that I will take to my grave. Yes, you see now how I am talented at wordplay! A sum of money has been lost. Lost. Yes. Lost forever."

He began to tear the papers. Why did he need them anyway? The words were already locked in his memory. They could *not* be lost! *Surely* God would not allow... "I will make no halt. I will be received by the Lady of the Mansion in the breakfast room. Breakfast is so intimate... I recall the promise lately given to Father. Where is the artillery? I was promised artillery. No mind. The battle is lost. Forever... Leyland, teacher of my art, there is a lady about whom I had such high hopes. I wait each day, breathless. But I am surrounded by powerful persons who hate me. And *she* is lost... Lydia, teacher of my heart, I had such high hopes of you. I wait and wait. But you are lost. I never hoped for your husband's death. Never. I swear. I never hoped for him to be lost. I hope only for honour and respect for every degree, kind and appetite... Powerful persons... Watching me..."

He reached into the bottom drawer, took out the small blue bottle. "Though they hate me, they will not tear from my heart the thousand recollections. They will not take from me the sunlight." His voice grew. "Do not let me be lost, O Great Editor. Do *not* let me be lost, O Father!" He uncorked the bottle. "Also, I had written a poem, and a novel which I have now lost. Lost. Forever lost. Where, where..? I can find nothing! I therefore wait each day, breathless." His voice rose again, almost a shriek. "And I have been waiting so long, Father! So very long!" He took a long drink from the bottle and dropped it empty.

Then he banged his fists on the desk top. One-two-three, one-two-three, one-two-three, one-two-three. He held his head in his hands and began to cry. He fell back into the chair and slumped head first on the desk. In the rest of the house there was silence.

DAYLIGHT SEEPED in the edges of the curtains. Charlotte was pummelling his shoulder, shouting at him: "Brother, brother, be awake!"

There was no response.

Her voice rose. "Brother! Brother! Be awake!"

She touched him. There was nothing. She shook him. There was nothing. She screamed.

THE TUNE was running through Patrick's head long before the congregation actually started singing:
"O God, our help in ages past,
Our hope for years to come,
Our shelter from the stormy blast,
And our eternal home.
Under the shadow of Thy throne
Still may we dwell secure;
Sufficient is Thine arm alone,
And our defence is sure.
Before the hills in order stood,
Or earth received her frame,

From everlasting Thou art God,
To endless years the same."

The singing faded. The organ trailed away. Patrick heard only the birdsong now as the coffin was lowered. He addressed the congregation: "In the midst of life..." He choked a little then continued: "We are here to mourn but also to celebrate. We celebrate a life of talent and richness. We celebrate my daughter Charlotte, a life lived fully and in God's grace." He opened the Bible. "The lesson for today is from Job, Chapter 1, verse 21: *Naked came I out of my mother's womb and naked shall I return thither...*"

A yard or so away stood John Brown. He leaned on his shovel. A voice ran through his head. It said: "Mourn. Celebrate. Talent. Richness. Grace. Lesson. What do words mean? They mean anything. They mean nothing."

Patrick spoke more loudly now. *"The Lord gave and the Lord hath taken away..."*

"Give and take away!" said the voice in John Brown's head, "Addition and subtraction! The sums go on forever!"

"Blessed be the name of the Lord." Patrick closed the heavy Bible and clasped it in his arms. "Charlotte was the final child of mine to die. Not one of them was spared to his allotted span. Yet Charlotte has given the world her words..."

The voice in John Brown said: "Writers! Poets! What do they know? They fret and posture and pretend they give us meaning. But they give us only their madness..."

Patrick was coming over to him. He heard Patrick's voice. "Do your work, Brown. I will leave you now. I must converse with the mourners, with those who loved her. I must speak with Mrs Gaskell before she leaves. She is preparing an account of Charlotte's life and the lives of her brother and sisters. So those lives will not be unknown, will not be in vain. For that we must be grateful."

John Brown stepped over to the grave and began to shovel the pile of earth. His voice said: "Grateful? Nay, I am not grateful. I shall take comfort only in inches, ounces, gallons, the stuff of measuring. Because it is they give the only truth to this life, those things that yield measurement." He stopped shovelling. He looked across to where Patrick mingled with the mourners. His voice said: "It has been hard for thee, parson. All thy chickens dead. But what were they in the end but quantities, volumes, lengths, weights, capacities? A Branwell or a Charlotte? What is the difference? And are the rest of us not the same?" When Patrick looked across at him he resumed his shovelling. "Tha's lost thy children. I will be thy child. Tha's lost a son. I will be thy son. Tha's lost a wife. I will be thy wife." He dropped the spade and opened his arms.

The voice continued: "For what is that final number, that infinity of all the infinities? It is six foot by six foot by two. I tell you this: every day I dig and every day I spend my hours measuring the world. And what is poetry? Only measures and metre. And what is music? Only numbers. One two three, one two three, one two three! One two three, one two three, one two three!"

After a while, when he saw the mourners had disappeared into the parsonage, he clenched his fists.

"She should have danced!" The voice was out now, out of his head. The voice was alive and in the world. "She should have danced with me! She should not have refused!"

He stood stock still, repeatedly clenching and unclenching his fists. He held out his arms, thought again of the slender waist and soft flesh.

Then he began to dance, round and round the graveyard. "One two three! One two three! One two three, Miss Emily! One two three! One two three, One two three!"

Oh yes. The numbers. The numbers lived on.

The Navigator's Daughter

THEY CAME out of the Woodhead Tunnel with a WHOOOOOSSHH! on the Sheffield side, the rattle-tat-tat of the train dying of a sudden, buried in the acres of light and space and passengers' voices flooding into the compartment with the relief of their escape.

Alice, her mother, said: "You mark that, Maudie, mark it well. Your grandad was a nipper when they built that tunnel, fetching and carrying for the excavators. *His* dad died of the cholera with 30 others that was buildin' it and your grandad was the man of the family then. Oh, such a man he was!" And she smiled her tight, knowing smile, hiding her uneven yellow teeth, and her eyes grew bright with the vision of Grandad Corner, a boy of nine, as though she herself had lived it, seen the very moment of her father's leap to manhood. But Maudie, barely nine herself, who had only known him from the bundle of brown photographs, could not reconcile this vision with the images she knew: a thin, dark, brooding man with heavy moustaches, bowler hat, waistcoat and kerchief, leaning on his shovel, his free arm bent and resting on his hip; or ramrod straight, a clay pipe in his mouth, hands in pockets, corduroy leggings tied with string; in both pictures unsmiling, unblinking, unchanging as the rock had been before he and his like drilled and shovelled it.

"It's good," said Alice, "to be goin' home." She bent down and kissed Maudie and hugged her.

"*Are* we goin' home?" asked Maudie, confused. "Are we *really*? Is our dad gonna be there?"

"Nay," said Alice, "Our *real* 'ome, I mean. Where we come from. Where your uncle Albert lives."

Maudie could not remember her Uncle Albert. She thought again of her dad, with his watery blue eyes and wispy blond moustache, of the house in Ancoats with the boarded window and the bird table her dad had made for the little garden. He had carried the breadcrumbs out in a newspaper and she had been excited to see a story about a new planet being discovered. It was called Pluto. She wanted to ask her dad about the new planet, but there were other things on his mind. He was saying – shouting – to Alice: "What do you mean by it? What do you bloody mean? I treated you right, didn't I? An' you shat on me, that's a fact! What a fool I've been, what a bloody fool! An' I don't suppose it's the first time...!"

"Nay," her mother had shouted back, "An' it won't be the last! Treated me right, did tha? Tha's not treated us like a *man*'d treat us! *Tha's* not a man! Tha can't keep tha women!" And she started to sing "*...the night that I told you those little white lies*" which was a new song she'd learned and taught Maudie, and she wagged her finger at Maudie's dad and laughed.

"If you go through that door, you needn't look to come back! You nor the lass! I'm warning you, Alice!"

"Warnin' *me*!" And she laughed again and tossed her fine chestnut hair and turned and took Maudie's hand – Maudie that was already in her tweed coat and woollen bonnet – and picked up the canvas bag in which she'd packed her underclothes, her blue Sunday dress and the photographs of Grandad Corner, and strode through the scullery and out the back door and down to the bus stop.

"*Him* warnin' *me*!" she kept saying all the way to Victoria Station, "Did you ever hear of such a thing?" She began to sing under her breath: "*Ooooh, love me or leave me...*" And then she laughed and Maudie laughed too, though she still thought about the bird table and the new planet. "Now," said Alice when they got on the train, "It's thee an' me, the two of us, now an' always, does tha understand?" She lit a cigarette and blew smoke out of the window at the trees and buildings skimming by, at the smoke and steam of the engine on the other side of the glass. "We'll be seein' your uncle Albert right soon. You've not seen him since you were small."

"SINCE YOU were small!" said Alice, "It's been thee an' me, the two of us. You know how much I love my home. *Our* home. I *do*. I don't like bein' away. I don't like being 'ere!" She tried to wave an arm to indicate it all, the awfulness around her, the long echoey ward, the nets and screens and muscular nurses, the old women slumped in armchairs with their mouths hanging open and their eyes empty of sense, the girl's voice on the radio singing something about a *material girl* whatever that was, but she overbalanced with the effort and Maudie rushed to help her, lifted her back onto the pillows, brushed the stringy white hair out of her eyes.

"You'll be allright, mam," she said, "They wouldn't keep you in if they didn't need to, now would they?"

"*Wouldn't* they?" Alice smiled a wild smile, displaying the unnatural whiteness of her dentures, "Oh wouldn't they? Well, let me tell you...." And she was off again – complaints about the food, the things they put *in* the food that they thought she didn't know about, the noise, the smell, the other women, so awful, but at least you could understand it with *them*, why *they* were in here. They were sick – two bricks short of a load, most of them. "But there's nowt wrong wi' *me*, lass. You know that, Maudie. Nowt wrong that being 'ome wouldn't cure!"

"She'll not get better," said the sister when Maudie talked to her in the office afterwards. "You must be prepared for that."

"I don't expect miracles," said Maudie, "But you'll have to tell me straight – how long has she got?"

"No, no, that's not what I mean. She could go on for years. I just mean she'll not get better. She'll have times like today when she's not too poorly, when she knows you and talks to you and remembers things and makes sense. Periods of remission, we call them. But they'll get shorter, less frequent. And the other times..." She glanced at the report on her desk. "The shaking and trembling, the falling down, messing herself, forgetting what you've told her two minutes before, telling lies, obsessive behaviour..."

"First it was sweets and cakes and things," said Maudie, "I'd come home and find the drawers full of barley sugars and chocolate buttons. Like a kid, she was. I didn't know whether to laugh or cry. And now she washes her hair five, six times a day when she's at home. I hide the shampoo but she uses Fairy Liquid..."

"We'll give you some tablets for the trembling so she should be able to feed herself, and some for the bowels and some others to make her sleep. Now, has anybody spoken to you about attendance allowance?"

"We've always managed before. We've both got our pensions and there's no rent or..." Maudie hesitated as realisation sank in. "You mean she's coming home again? Permanent?"

"There's nothing more we can do. And there are so many old people these days, we just don't have the beds. The only alternative, you realise, is some kind of mental institution, and I'm sure..."

"Oh no, no. I'd never do that."

"Now – this attendance allowance. It could be twenty pounds a week. Not to be sniffed at. And she *wants* to go home, talks about nothing else. And it *might* do some good, you never can tell. Oh, she wants to go home allright, drives us batty with it..."

"I WANT TO GO HOME!" said Maudie, "You promised!" She tugged at Alice's skirt.

"I've got just the song for you, lass." said Alice. She had opened the piano stool and was glancing through the sheet music, humming a snatch of *Yessir, That's My Baby*! or *Sleepytime Gal*. Now she started singing "*Shoooow me the way to go 'ome, I'm tired and I wanna go to bed...*"

"I'm sorry," said Albert, loudly, breaking in, "I'm sorry. I've done all I can." You could tell he was Alice's brother: same hair, almost copper now in the sunlight through the big bay window, and the same way of standing – head forward, shoulders back, feet apart – when he was trying to make a point.

Alice stopped in mid-chorus. "It's that Dorothy, that bloody wife o' thine! With her airs and graces an' bloody piano! She's turned thee agin us!"

"Nay, nay," he shook his head glumly, "Tha knows what trouble is! If thee an' that Frank had done right an' proper thing before the bairn came along..."

"She never liked us, that Dorothy. Well, I suppose when tha marries brass, there's not much love lost."

"It's not that. It's not Dorothy. It's just... I've a position now, and with our own bairn ont' way..."

"If our dad could hear thee now, he'd take off his belt to thee!"

"Don''t go on about our dad!"

"Nay, I don't suppose it does much for thy position."

"Look, look," Albert took her by the shoulders but she broke away, threw the music across the room so that Maudie, excited now, caught some sheets as they floated down. "There's no room here, not with bairn ont' way. Tha can see for thyssen. But there is an 'ouse."

"Where?"

"Attercliffe. Near the station. Oh, I don't say it's much, but it's summat. It's one of a pair that Dorothy's dad had gid 'im by way of settlement for a debt. We don't expect rent mind, not till tha gets on thy feet again."

"Tha'll get what's due when I've got it to give." Alice picked Maudie up and kissed her. "Maudie an' me pay us way, don't we, duck?"

"Oh, Alice," said Albert, "Why'd you leave him, lass? He seemed a nice enough lad, did Frank."

"The world's full o' nice lads. It's men that's scarce. Men that'll stick by you an' not wittle on about their position."

Albert sighed. "Tha'll be needing some brass to tide thee over, I dare say." He took two ten shilling notes from his trouser pocket. "Look, it's not a bad 'ouse, tha knows. Thee'll like it, Maudie. It's got little angels carved int' corners of the ceiling int' parlour. Little cherr-abims. Oh, lovely little angels..."

"SEE THOSE LITTLE ANGELS?" said Tom. He held Maudie high in the air. "See those little angels up ont' ceiling? They're like thee, Maudie. Thee's my little angel!" He kissed her, dropped her back into the patched armchair, making her drop her pencil.

"Leave the girl alone," said Alice, "Leave our Maudie alone." She was putting on her make-up in the big oblong gilt-edged looking glass.

"Jealous?" asked Tom. He put his arm round Alice's waist, "Tha's no need to be. Maudie's my little angel, but thee's ma big 'un! Thee's a beauty!" And he kissed her on the neck.

"None o' your sauce! Oh, now you've smudged us!" She slapped his hand which lay across her shoulder and he shook it and blew on it and danced across the width of the small sitting room, making out it hurt. "Oh, oh, I don't know what I'll do! Oh, tha's done for me, Alice!"

"Tha's a babby!" said Alice, "an' tha'll always *be* a babby! Now stop lekkin' about for a minute!"

Tom settled down in the second of the two armchairs, across the hearth from Maudie, and winked at her. He had the *face* of a baby – round, smooth, hardly a shadow of a whisker. Maudie smiled and turned back to the exercise book resting on her knee. After a while, she said: "How d'you turn fractions into decimals, Uncle Tom?"

"That's summat they don't teach us ont' coalface," he said, "*We've* no need of it. Can't do sums int' dark. Now I'm a grafter down there, by God I am, but yer mam makes us work a damn sight harder up here an' no mistake!" He reached across the deal table covered in the *News of the World* and picked up the Woodbines and the Swan Vestas. "Lessee what I've gone an' done today to earn this bit o' rest." He glanced across to make sure Alice was listening. "I've cleaned the grate, I've scrubbed the kitchen floor. I've cut up the *Mail* an' hung it int' privy," – Maudie giggled at this – "I've rubbed us shoes wi' lard to make 'em shine an' squeal like new, good enough to go to church in, though the only place yer mam wants to go on Sunday is the pub. Lekkin', she says!" He lit a cigarette and threw the spent match at the fire but it hit the grate, bounced, landed on the floorboards an inch away from the peg rug. He bent down quickly to pick it up. "Don't want to burn your mam's rug." He raised his voice. "I don't think she's noticed, preenin' herself in front o' glass. Tha wouldn't tell on me, would tha, Maudie? Tha wouldn't tell 'er what I done?"

"You know I wouldn't," said Maudie. She giggled again.

"Ay, I do. I know tha's straight an' wouldn't give me away. An' I know tha's clever too."

"Don't think I don't know what goes on," said Alice. She straightened the jacket of her black velvet costume and turned away from the glass. "How do I look, Tom Dutton? Here, give us a puff."

He handed her the cigarette. "You look like a film star."

"You look like that Marlene Dietrich, mam."

"Even better," said Tom, "more life-like."

"Well, stir thyssen or we'll miss the bus. It's always the same, gobbin' wi' our Maudie, tellin' her she's clever. It won't do her no good, turning 'er 'ead like that. She'll just go on sittin' on 'er backside all day writin' things."

Maudie looked up quickly. "It's for school, mam."

"You'll need glasses soon and then where'll you be? You're no beauty queen *now*."

"She doesn't allus do sums," said Tom, "She writes poetry, don't you, lass?"

Maudie shot him a glance. "Only for school."

"You do too much for school," Alice gave Tom the cigarette back. "A lot of good school ever did for the likes of us. Oh, I know who gives you grand ideas – if it's not Tom, it's our Dorothy. I've never liked that woman and she don't like us. The only reason she's taken to you is she's got no bairns of her own and not likely to 'ave since she lost that first 'un."

"Oh, mam..."

"Tha knows I say these things for thy own good, duck. Now, there's plenty o' tea an' some fresh cheese int' pantry an' some o' them arrowroot biscuits you're partial to. See, I look after thee, Maudie. Gi' us a kiss then."

Maudie kissed her. After Alice and Tom had gone, she went up to her bedroom and burrowed beneath the bed, bringing out an orange exercise book identical to the first. She stood by the window overlooking the yards with their washing lines, their privies and their pigeon coops silhouetted in the growing dusk. She began to read aloud: "*The World is a Star*, by Maude Corner, Aged 11." She coughed.

"*The world is a star,*
Seen by other stars,
Aglow with itself
And the people on it.

"*The world is a star,*
But I only see
The light of other stars
Falling on me.

63

"The world is a star,
Brilliant in space,
Beautiful to watch
From some other place."

After a while – it had grown really dark by now – she put the exercise book back under the bed and went downstairs to mash some tea in the kitchen.

THE MEN came out of the kitchen. Cyril was grinning. Fit to bust, as Alice would say. The other two looked subdued. "Well," said Cyril, "that were a reet good neet."

"Expensive night," said one of the others – a thin, pale-faced man in a grey suit that had seen better days.

"Unlucky night," said the other, who wore overalls.

"Unlucky for some," said Cyril, "But we all get a run o' bad luck now and again an' all we can do is 'ave a little patience an' wait while it ends. Alice! Maudie! Say goodnight to my pals – they're just off now."

Alice got up from the armchair where she was reading *Red Letter* and turned off Jack Hylton on the wireless. Maudie looked up from the hearthrug where she was crayoning the pictures in the *News Chronicle Royal Family Colouring Book*. "Goodnight," they said.

"Goodnight," said the men and Cyril showed them out. "Twenty-five pound!" he shouted when he closed the door, "Twenty-five pound in a night! Hah! Bloody fools!" He guffawed, clapped his hands, pulled at his braces and did a little jig. "Come on, Alice girl! Bring out a bottle! We've got summat to celebrate an' we can afford it tonight!"

Alice brought the Johnny Walker out of the closet on the landing. Cyril went back to the kitchen, came out again with some glasses and his crown and anchor board. "Here, lass – this little board has worked a treat tonight. Come on, Alice – touch it for luck. You too, Maudie."

Maudie put down her crayon, leaving the Prince of Wales – *The Man Born to Be King* – with hair half yellow, half white. She walked slowly across to Cyril and touched the crown square quickly, nervously, with just the tip of a finger.

"Ay up," said Cyril, "It won't bite, tha knows. It's good, it's nice. Nice Board, nice to us tonight. Go on. Touch it proper." Suddenly his mood changed, his voice was angry. "Touch it like you'd touch a lad you was courting, all soft an' loving an' gentle like. Else you know what you'll get."

"I won't have talk like that," said Alice, "Not wi' a lass *her* age. It's not right."

"Gerraway! She'll be left school next year, but she's not too old for me to take me belt off to! An' neither is thee!"

"Go on," said Alice, "Go on, Maudie. Do as Uncle Cyril says. For your mam's sake, eh?"

Maudie touched it again, slowly this time, brushing the surface with all four fingers. Cyril laughed, his good humour returned. "Shouldn't wonder if tha's not got a lad already," he said.

"I haven't," said Maudie, and, turning to Alice, "Honest."

"Course not," said Alice, "Thee an' me's got no secrets, have we, duck? And I don't know what you've brought three glasses for, Cyril Turton. I'll not have you start my daughter off on strong drink."

"Eh, come on, Alice, it's a special night!" He twirled his heavy ginger moustache in a comic music hall gesture, then poured out three glasses of the whisky, using the crown and anchor board as a tray. "Come on now. People say there's a bloody depression on, people marchin' from bloody Jarrow, but I say there's always a bit o' brass to be med and if there was a few more smart lads like me around, Mr Baldwin wouldn't have no problems. Let's drink to clever blokes like me, Alice."

"Don't go chuckin' it away now you've med it," said Alice, "I dunno – you're a right 'un! You can do owt when you set your mind to it. You can make *us* do owt."

Afterwards, with the warmth of the whisky inside her, Maudie took a candle and went out to the privy. She put on a new sanitary towel, wrapped the used one in a newspaper and carried it back to the house. She would throw it on the fire first chance she got. Back in the kitchen, she washed her face and hands at the sink, then went upstairs. She undressed in the dark with the bedroom curtains open and put on her long nightgown with the lace at the neck.

Once in bed, she found, as usual, that she couldn't sleep. She was waiting for the sounds. Every night she waited for the sounds of Alice and Cyril from the front bedroom, knowing that if she fell asleep beforehand, she would only be woken up when they came to bed. Tonight she had to wait even longer than usual. It was the whisky, of course. And when they finally came up, she could tell from the tenor of their voices that it had turned nasty, as Alice would say. The drink had turned it nasty. These times were the worst because, instead of the giggling, the fumbling, the little cries, the strange liquid sounds, instead of these would come the thuds, the muffled squeals of fear and pain, the flood of Cyril's anger reaching its climax. And afterwards, Alice's weeping, far into the morning, and the foolish stories to explain the bruising in the light of tomorrow.

Tonight, as Maudie listened to them undressing, their unintelligible whispers hung over her like a threat she could not properly define. Then the voices ceased. Then there was only quiet. Surely, they had not fallen asleep already? But perhaps the whisky had had more than its usual effect on Cyril. Perhaps... she was falling asleep herself when she was suddenly aware of a shadow in the moonlight.

"Shouldn't wonder if tha's not got a lad already," said Cyril. He was naked except for his vest. He held his trouser belt in his right hand, slapping his left palm gently, almost caressingly...

"I haven't. Honest."

"Don't reckon I'll have need of this then." He put his belt on the pillow next to her face so she could feel the coldness of the buckle on her skin. "Tell me you're goin' to be a good girl, Maudie. Tell me I'll 'ave no need to chastise you."

'No! Oh, no!'

"That's good." He laughed. "Come on, Maudie, touch it for luck. It won't bite, tha knows. It's nice. Touch it proper, all soft an' lovin' like you'd touch the lad you're courtin'." And he laughed again and lowered himself on top of her, crushing her with the weight of him.

SHE WAS crushed between Alice and Aunt Dorothy. Everyone was singing, but Maudie didn't know the words. She moved her lips to show willing. They had been singing *Underneath the Arches*, which was one of the few songs she knew and which was a bit of a joke really because that was where the shelter was – underneath the railway arches on The Wicker. There were about a hundred people there tonight and they could hear the thunder of the bombs, see the flashes light up the buildings, smell the smoke. They could have stayed at home in Attercliffe, used a shelter there, but Alice liked to come into Sheffield early and visit Dorothy. "Now that Albert's out fire-watching, she'll be in need of company." And Dorothy always gave them a glass of sherry before the sirens went off. The song they were singing now was a new one, something about moonlight going with your hair. Maudie adjusted her glasses nervously.

She had been sitting there two hours already and she felt stiff in her legs and back as well as hot and sticky. In the early days she had brought along a book – *The Citadel* or *The Ragged Trousered Philanthropists* or *Howard's End*, the books that Barry recommended. But the crush of the crowd and the noise had always prevented her reading.

It seemed a lifetime, but it always passed. First there would be the lull with people growing expectant and the odd voice proclaiming: "That's it then. Must be over." The singing would peter out and they would wait, quiet and alert, for the all-clear. After that, it was T'ra, Goo'bye, Alsithee, Same time, same place. Laughter. Oh that's a good'un. That's a deaf'un.

"Well," said Alice when they got back to Dorothy's, "it weren't so bad."

"I'll get us another sherry," said Dorothy, "to strengthen our nerves." She was a square-faced woman with dyed blonde hair. "You light the gas for us, Maudie."

Maudie lit the fire and they sat down on the three-piece. "Poor Maudie," said Dorothy when she came back, "You'll need some sleep if you're workin' tomorrow. Though it's not really tomorrow, o' course, it's today."

"She'll be allright, will Maudie. She's a strong lass like her mam. Strong like her grandad Corner."

"You can stay the night here, both of you. There's room enough."

"No," said Maudie, "I've got things at home I've got to take into work."

"Who'd've thought it – a daughter of mine workin' ont' twist drill at Balfour's? Doin' man's work!" Alice fairly exploded with mirth.

"And only getting' paid half what a man gets!" said Maudie angrily.

"Well, what do you expect? You're only there till the men come back. You make the most of it, lass! You know, Dot, we've got more money comin' into that 'ouse than we ever had before, what wi' Maudie at Balfour's an' me makin' brushes at 'ome. I don't know what we ever needed men for, I don't. Really." She giggled and took another sip of her sherry.

"You talk as if you like this war," said Dorothy, "You talk as if you enjoy it."

"Nay, nay, I don't say that. But I do say it's got its compensations. Oh, I know there's folk getting' killed, good men an' strong men, an' more's the pity. But people are always dyin', aren't they? If it's not one thing, it's another. An' I do say this – people are more together when there's a war on, don't you think? More friendly. Like int' shelter tonight – all that singin'. Everybody likes a bit o' singin'. Everybody joined in."

"Ay," said Dorothy, "All together. Joining in. I'll give you that."

"Mind you, we've always had that, Maudie an' me, war or no war. I mean it's always been the two of us, girls together, lookin' after each other. We've never needed owt else, isn't that right, Maudie? D'you know, some people don't take us for mother an' daughter, they take us for sisters. Isn't that funny? Ta, Dot – I *will* have another if you don't mind. I think I'll have a fag too. I like a smoke with my drink, I do. That's the only thing I don't like about them shelters – they don't let you smoke. Course, we can all see the reason. Still... What about you, Maudie? Do you want another drink? Maudie? Oh, look what I've done, I've gone and spilt some."

"Poor lass, she's asleep. Well, that settles it, Alice. You'll have to stay the night now."

"Tell me if it's none of my business, Dot, but where do you an' Albert get this Spanish sherry? I'm right partial to a medium sweet..."

"DON'T TELL me to mind my own business! Don't talk to your mother like that! You're not too old to get a good hiding off me, my girl! The way I should've done when you were little, the way your *grandad* would've done! Oh, I blame the place you're workin' in – it's given thee ideas above thyssen. Though I can't see it lastin' much longer – there's plenty of lads comin' home lookin' for work an' tha's best make up tha mind to find thyssen a decent chap as'll treat thee proper an' see thee stay at home and 'ave bairns."

"But I've *got* a chap, mam. And he *is* decent and proper!"

"Decent and proper and *married*! Which means he's only decent an' proper with woman he's married to!"

"He's getting a divorce."

"Divorce! Is he then? How long's he been tellin' you that? Three years, is it? Three years you've been carryin' on an' I never knew about it! I wouldn't know today if it weren't for that Dorothy! Oh, that woman's been waitin' for summat like this an' now it's come! You should've seen 'er! Smile like a Cheshire cat! That's what hurts as much as owt – her bein' the one that telled me!"

"She had no right."

"She had *every* right. She's your auntie."

"Well, it makes no difference."

"It makes a difference to *me*, lass!"

"I don't see why it should. You an' your men!" Maudie's voice rose to a scream. "How many is it, mam, or have you never tallied up?"

Alice slapped her so hard her head snapped back and she nearly fell. She burst into tears and Alice hugged her. "Oh Maudie, just look at thyssen. You're twenty-six and know nowt. You know nowt about *men* at any rate, or you wouldn't be in this scrape. Men? I've had men allright, but not one as I knew were married, not one as I knew were married when I met 'im. What's he do, this Barry? Senior draughtsman, is it? What's that when it's at 'ome? It's not a *man's* job. I'll senior draughtsman 'im! Does his wife know?"

"Course she does," said Maudie in between sobs, "Course she knows."

"*I* bet!"

"She knows, I tell you. They don't get on, haven't got on for years, long before him an' me..."

"And there's bairns?"

"There's only Anthony. He's seven. Barry and his wife, they've not had... relations. Not for years."

"Appen e's been doin' allright for hissen all the same."

"It's the child we're waiting on. Till he's older and can understand..."

"Well, *I* understand, my girl, and I'll tell you what we're going to do. I'll get me coat an' we'll go round and 'ave a little talk with *Missus* Senior Draughtsman an' find out what she really knows an' what she's got to say for 'erself."

"Mam!"

"Come on, luv. Come on, Maudie. I'm goin' by myssen if I 'ave to, but it's best if tha sees for thyssen which way the wind blows. It's all fort' best, I promise. Oh, come on, Maudie, come on, girl!"

"COME ON, MAM, ELSE WE'LL BE LATE!"

"I didn't think it started at half past seven," said Alice, "I thought it were eight o'clock. I swear it said eight o'clock int' *Star*, Maudie, I'm sure it did."

"No," said Maudie, "I *told* you when it was starting. I told you *both*. Now we're late for the bus."

"Well," said Arthur, "I don't mind. I were only goin' for thy sake, Alice. I don't get to t' pictures much. Well, you can see it all on telly these days." He went across to the chrome-edged convex mirror by the door, brushed his thin grey hair with his hand, stroked his pepper and salt moustache.

"Don't say that. Not after all the trouble Maudie went to, missin' her evening class. You'd enjoy it, I expect. It's a good film."

"Ow d'you know?" asked Arthur triumphantly. He wagged a finger at Alice. "Ow d'you know it's a good film if you've not seen it? Tell us, go on. Eh, I've got you there, girl."

"Because everybody said it's good." Alice slumped down on the settee and kicked off her shoes. "It's Alfred Hitchcock. Everybody knows *he's* good, Alfred Hitchcock. And it's got that actor in it, 'im that's very thin."

"Anthony Perkins," said Maudie, "Well, I suppose we're not going. You light the gas fire, mam, and I'll make us some coffee."

"I never knew they wouldn't let you in once the picture started though. I've never 'eard that one before. Have you, Arthur? I've never 'eard o' that."

"I don't go much, at all, love. Hutch up." He settled on the seat beside her and unbuckled his belt. "There, that's better."

"Tha's putting on weight. Tha'll 'ave to go on a diet."

"Nay, I'm just well built. Don't you go naggin' me. Now, what's this night school Maudie's goin' to?'

"She's learning shorthand. So she can be a secretary. Well, they all need shorthand these days. And she's wasted with what she's doin' now. Just filin' things an' writin' in ledgers. She's wasted. She's got brains, allright. I've *always* said that. But she's never used 'em. She should've stayed on at school but she never did. You need qualifications these days for everything. And she's no spring chicken any more."

"She should've wed. I don't hold wi' women working."

"Don't let Maudie catch you saying *that*. Bit late in the day for that! But you're right, duck, she's wasted herself wi' men as well. Not like her mam." Alice squeezed Arthur's hand and he gave a short, excited laugh. Then Maudie came in with the cups.

"Here. Give us one, duck. Ooh 'eck...!" As Alice took the cup, she spilled some of the coffee. "Oh, look at that! This carpet shows every stain. We could do with a new one, one o'them Persian carpets like Dorothy's got, wall to wall. She won't like that. She doesn't like other people 'avin' same as she's got. Oh, get us a rag, there's a good girl. We can afford a new carpet, can't we?"

"I suppose," said Maudie, returning with a dishcloth, "Here, I'll do it, mam. Tell Arthur his coffee's there. Don't let *him* knock it over too."

"What do you think about the carpet, Arthur? We've been in this 'ouse, Maudie an' me, since she were a kid, you know, but it's *your* 'ouse now as much as it's... Well, look at that. Just look at that. He's asleep. Just like that. Dead to the world."

"He's tired, mam, he's old."

"Old? He's not *old*. He's *my* age. I won't 'ave 'im old!" She jabbed her elbow into Arthur's side. "Wake up, you silly old bugger!"

He woke with a start. "What? What? Are we goin' then? Are we goin' after all?"

"Nay," said Alice, "if we went, tha'd likely fall asleep an' we might not be able to wake thee an' tha's such a fat lump, it'd take four men to carry thee 'ome."

FOUR MEN from Forgemasters carried the coffin, though Arthur had been retired six years. Their wreath said: *Goodbye to one of the best*.

"Well," said Alice, "if he were one o' the best, I never found out what 'e were best at. If he were one o' the best, I'd 'ate to meet one o' the worst, that's all *I* can say."

"Hush, mam," said Maudie.

"I will *not*."

"Tell her to hush, Aunt Dorothy."

"Maudie's right. Don't make a scene. You were very good at *Albert's* funeral."

"Albert was allright wi' us. Left us the 'ouse, didn't he? Oh, Albert was a good man like 'is dad. But this one – he'd not been a man since... since I can't remember. I *can't*. Tell 'er, Maudie. Tell 'er I'm speakin' truth."

"Please, mam."

"I'm well rid, I don't mind tellin' you. Just Maudie an' me now, like it always was. And if this lot think they're comin' back for ham sandwiches, they're very much mistaken. We've nowt int' fridge anyway. And I don't know 'ayf on 'em. I wouldn't mind if they was kin, but 'e had no blood relatives 'cept for a second cousin in Clitheroe."

"It'll be just us," said Maudie, "You and me and Aunt Dorothy. We'll sit down with a piece of cake and a glass of sherry and remember him. He wasn't *that* bad, mam."

"I'm not very keen on sherry, luv. Have we not got some Johnny Walker left over from Christmas?" Afterwards, back at the house, she said: "I suppose I'll miss 'im though. I do like these Benson and Edges, Dot. Pass us the ash tray, Maudie, there's a good girl. You do miss people, don't you? Funny 'ow you do."

"I'VE BEEN missing it three days," said Maudie, "And the money's been drawn."

"I know nowt," said Alice, "What're you saying? I've got to run."

Maudie waited in the front bedroom. Eventually the lavatory flushed and Alice came out onto the landing, alert, her head to one side like a hunted animal listening for pursuit.

"You took it," said Maudie, "You took it and you cashed it. My pension."

"I was goin' to tell you. I thought: *Save 'er the trouble, I'll do it for 'er when I get my own.* That's what I thought."

"But you never *did* tell me."

"I forgot."

"Where's the money then?"

"I forget. I mean, I get confused. It's in me purse. *One* of me purses. I don't remember which."

"You took it out of my dresser. Other things too. I'm not angry, mam, but I've got to know."

"No. You must've left it lying about. I did it to save you trouble, that's all. *What* other things?"

"Private things. Old things. Papers."

"Papers? Letters, you mean. Letters from that Harry."

"Old letters."

"*Dirty* letters. I read them, didn't I? Dirty. That's the only word to describe them. We shouldn't 'ave letters like that in our 'ouse. You shouldn't keep such letters."

"What've you done with my letters?"

73

"Burned 'em. Threw 'em away. I don't know. I forget."

Maudie strode across to the tallboy.

"My drawers!" shouted Alice, "Those are *my* drawers! You don't go in my drawers, madam!"

Maudie searched through the drawers while Alice stood and muttered. She found the letters and some school reports and some orange exercise books. "These belong to me," she said, "You took them."

"I never. He still writes, doesn't 'e? Your fancy man. You think I don't know but I do."

"No, he doesn't, mam, not since... They're old, mam, honest. He's never written since... You know. You remember."

"You blame *me*. You blame me for stopping it. But it weren't right. It weren't. I 'ad to."

"I don't blame you, mam. Really."

"I don't know why you're making all this fuss if you don't blame me. What's all the fuss about? *I* didn't take your letters."

"They're in your drawer, mam."

"You've no rights looking there."

"I just kept them, just to remember."

"And I've seen in *there*!" shouted Alice. She snatched at one of the exercise books. "I've seen what you've written. You ought to be ashamed, you ought. And you're the one supposed to 'ave brains, supposed to be educated! You're the one supposed to write poetry! Call this poetry?" She opened the book and read out: "*The last time I saw Paris, her heart was young and gay. You are my sunshine, my only sunshine. I don't want to set the world on fire, I just want to start a flame in your heart. That old black magic's got me in its spell...* oh, pages an' pages of it! The bloody book's full of it! Call that poetry?"

"I don't call it poetry, mam. They're names of songs, that's all." Maudie wiped her eyes.

"Names of songs? Course they're names of songs. Think I don't know that? I know *all* the songs, I do! I suppose they're the names of the songs you an' your fancy man liked!"

"I was never good at remembering songs."

"Poetry! You couldn't write poetry! You never could! Pages an' pages of names of songs! That's all you were good for writing! That's all!" Alice laughed, high and wild and desperate.

"I'm taking my things, mam. I'm going to my room."

"Oh Maudie, I'm sorry. I didn't mean to read 'em. I must've picked them up, tidied them away, picked them up by mistake where you'd dropped them. That must be it. Eh, Maudie..." She threw her arms round Maudie and began to cry softly. "I wouldn't do owt to hurt thee, lass. Honest. I love thee. I *do*. I just forget. I forget what I do with things. And these teeth. These new teeth don't fit right. I'm in pain, Maudie, all the time. I swear it."

"I know. I know. You've just got to wear them, then they'll get better." She put an arm round Alice's shoulder and kissed her forehead. Very gently, she prised the exercise book out of Alice's hand. "I know you forget things, mam."

'YOU'RE FORGETTIN' one thing!' shouted Alice, sitting up in bed, pointing, 'I *know* about you!'

"Shush, mam, don't be silly," said Maudie. There was a new girl on the radio. She sang: *Turn arou-ou-nd...*

"Oh I do, I do!" There were pillows at her back and a grey knitted blanket half on, half off the bed. "Oh yes, I do!"

"Course you do. You know *me*. I'm Maudie. But you don't want to shout. The nurses don't like it." She looked round to see if any of them were coming over. The girl sang: *Turn around, bright eyes...*

"I know all about you – tellin' people I'm going funny in the 'ead. Your own mother. Oh, they listen to you because you're la-did-dah. But I can see through it, through all your airs an' graces, young lady. An' I know why you do it, don't think I don't know!"

"Oh mam, don't!" Maudie couldn't bear it when Alice talked like this, couldn't get used to it, even though she knew it was part of the illness, the doctors had warned her, it didn't mean anything. "Don't talk that way! I love you!"

"I know why it is!" Alice looked round the ward to see who was listening. The old women, the ones who were really sick, the ones who *should* be there and no argument, propped up in their chairs, dribbling, you never knew about them, never knew whether they took anything in. She turned back to Maudie. "It's 'cause of 'im, isn't it?"

Maudie took out her handkerchief and blew her nose. The girl on the radio sang: *Forever's gonna start tonii-iiight....* It didn't help things when she cried. She wasn't *going* to cry. "I love you, mam," she said, "You're all I've got."

"You've had it on your mind all these years an' I don't care who knows it. Oh, I should've *known*, I should've known when Albert left the 'ouse to you instead of me. You made Albert think I was funny in the 'ead then, didn't you? You worked your wiles on 'im and 'e couldn't see through you." She looked round the ward again and smiled. Heads were turned her way, most of the heads that *could* turn, that is. "All these years!"

"It's your house too. It'll always be yours as much as it's mine. Please..."

"I *won't* shush. I don't care who 'ears!"

"I'll bring you a cup of tea. Would you like that?"

"I don't *want* cups of tea. I don't want *owt* from the likes of you. You've always 'ated me!"

"It's not true!"

"So now you think you're rid of me!"

"No, mam, you'll be home soon. I promise. You an' me. Like it always was. I'll look after you."

"You? Look after *me*? Who d'you think you are then? You've never 'ad what *I* 'ad! Never 'ad the looks! Never 'ad the men comin' round you like I 'ad! No, never! And it's because of 'im, isn't it? You've never forgiven me!"

"Yes I have, mam. You were right. He'd never have got that divorce. He was stringing me along. There, I've said it. I start to read those letters now and I think: *What a fool I must've been!* You're right − I never could get the men, could I? That's why I keep *them*, the letters. To remind me to be sensible. You were right about Barry. I know that now."

"Barry? Barry?" Alice's eyes glinted with suspicion. "Don't play innocent with me, my girl. Don't give me *Barry*. Who's this Barry?"

"Mam..."

"You always wanted 'im. Always comin' down in that bloody lace nightdress, showin' all you've got. Call that decent? Well, *I* don't! E was the only one, the only one out of all of them that was a *real* man, the only man as could 'old a candle to your grandad. Oh, I knew what was goin' on though. I knew you wanted 'im. What was 'e to do? E was a man with a man's feelings. And then 'e was gone, slung 'is 'ook like all the rest. My *Cyril*. But *I* was the one 'e wanted – not you! An' you've never forgiven me!"

"Mam..." Maudie's body went suddenly cold and she had to grip the iron rail round the bed to stop from falling. All around her, all along the ward, the old women in the chairs continued to stare and to dribble. She shut her eyes and opened them again and took a deep breath and let go. It was allright. She could stand. "I'll get it now," she said. Her voice was louder, higher, than she intended and she made an effort to control it. "I'll get you that cup of tea."

"I'll never forgive thee!" shouted Alice at her back.

"YOU'LL NEVER forgive yourself!" said Dorothy over the phone, "Leavin' your mother to rot in some loony bin. That's what it all boils down to. Oh, they call them by a lot of long words nowadays, but they're still loony bins. That's where they'll put her."

"I can't help it, Aunt Dorothy. I've made up my mind. I've got to have a life of my own."

"*Life of your own*? What're you talkin' about? You're sixty-three! Life of your own, indeed!"

Maudie put the phone down and looked round the living room. It was a good room, small but comfortable. It had changed so much since they first moved in a lifetime ago: the wall-to-wall carpet had taken them three years to pay for; the white Swedish leather suite had been a gift from Dorothy when she refurnished her own house from Uncle Albert's insurance; the stereo had been Alice's idea but she hardly ever played it because "there aren't any good songs nowadays" and the cabinet beside it was full of Maudie's *Classics for Pleasure*.

Maybe – it wasn't such an extravagance – maybe she could swop the black and white TV for a colour one this Christmas.

It was a good room, but it needed a bit of a tidy. She picked up the bundle of photographs she had been sorting through, the pictures of Grandad Corner – his dark, brooding face, his heavy moustaches, his waistcoat and his leggings and his bowler hat, and suddenly, with a passion that surprised her, she tore them in half and half again and dropped them, piece by piece, into the waste paper bin.

Suntdot

MR BERRY was late again. At least it was Friday. That was *some* consolation.

As he crossed the playground, he could hear the clearing of throats and the virile touch of Mr Duckworth (Maths) on piano. Each note boomed forth like a separate and studied achievement, an end in itself.

Mr Berry circled the annexe and arrived at the main entrance beneath the sign Castlefield Education Authority: Drivers Lane Secondary Modern School for Boys. He glanced briefly at his reflection in the glass panels of the door: his tie was straight; his sports coat fastened at the centre button; his hair, which normally obscured his forehead, was windswept and untidy but a quick brush with his hand would settle that.

Once again, he considered his plump, almost cherubic face and the undignified youthfulness it radiated. Not for the first time he considered growing a moustache. It would give him a certain gravitas, add a touch of maturity to his 23 years. But it was certain to take a long time and the others – boys and masters both – would stare at him and ask if he had forgotten to shave, and he would be filled with consternation in case the finished version should be an anti-climax. Best leave it then. Perhaps he should think about wearing glasses. Yes, that might be the answer.

He gripped his briefcase tightly, scraped his shoes on the metal grating, pushed open the door and wiped his feet again on the coconut mat inside. It had been raining and muddy all week. Mr Bateson (Geography) had been predicting snow. Mr Berry dropped his coat and briefcase off in the masters' cloakroom and slunk into the hall by the west door behind 5C. They glanced at him and grinned knowingly. Somehow he must reach his customary position at the end of 2B without Mr Crobert seeing him.

Mr Crobert, the headmaster, was in the centre of the stage, grasping the lectern piously, eyes bowed as the introduction died away. There was a pause for the intake of 600 breaths. Mr Duckworth's hands hovered for a second like arthritic birds of prey, then plummeted. Six hundred voices shuddered into life.

> *"A man that looks on glass*
> *On it may stay his eye*
> *Or if he pleaseth, through it pass*
> *And then the heav'n espy."*

Mr Berry was almost home when Dawson 3A stepped out of line with an urgent whispered "Sir!" and held out a hymn book. Mr Berry took it grudgingly. He had forgotten his own, but was annoyed that Dawson should assume as much. As it was, the movement caught Mr Crobert's eye and he fixed Mr Berry with a grim headmasterly expression. Mr Berry felt his face grow hot and he fumbled for Dawson's hymn book, dropping it. The singing, never more than ragged, trailed off into mumbles at the end of a verse.

"Boys," said Mr Crobert, testing the word. "Boys," hugging the lectern with his scrawny arms and leaning like a vulture into the first form rows. "BOYS!" much louder now, straightening up, adjusting his gown, taking one step backwards. He was a tall, angular, sharp-featured man with thinning grey hair brushed back and greased against his reddened scalp. His hawk-like nose and square jaw were made for imparting a sense of authority. "I know it's the end of the week. I realise you've been working hard. Baverstock 2A – I'll take that conker away from you if you don't stop playing with it. But I think we can put a lot more effort into our singing. In fact, I *know* we can. Now – I want you all to take a good look at the cover of your hymn book."

The boys all looked at the cover of their hymn book. Mr Crobert gave them plenty of time. Then he held up his own.

"You all see this printing on the front, the lettering on the cover, the title of the hymn book?"

They nodded. They saw.

"And what," asked Mr Crobert, "does it say?"

"Hymn book," suggested Groves 1B and was mercifully ignored.

"Songs of Praise," said most of the school.

"Songs of Praise," repeated Mr Crobert. A satisfied smile spread over his face, revealing to those in the first few rows yellow teeth with an edging of brown. "PRAISE!" he had pressed the volume button again. "We know what that means. don't we? Praise is a joyful, enthusiastic word. Isn't that so?" That thrusting jaw challenged them to contradict. They declined to do so. "So let us try to *sound* joyful and enthusiastic when we're praising the Lord. I know the weather's not very bright. It's a miserable day and we're all miserable. It's the end of the week and we're tired. *I'm* tired. *You're* tired. I'm sure Mr *Duckworth* is tired." Mr Crobert waved a hand at the surprised pianist who was spitting into his handkerchief, "and he's thinking about all the things he'll be doing over the weekend. A spot of gardening, I shouldn't wonder. And I suppose Kitchener 3X – who has spent the last five minutes talking to the boy next to him and will be seeing me in my room after assembly – wants to go to the football match tomorrow. Your team is Leeds United, I believe, Kitchener?"

Kitchener nodded and looked down at his feet. The school hooted approval. Their headmaster knew the name of a football team and his enemies were vanquished.

"Well then," Mr Crobert sensed his victory, "We're all thinking how hard we've worked and how we've earned the right to enjoy ourselves this weekend. Work and enjoyment. Two things for which we must praise the Lord. So let's have some enthusiasm. And remember to sound those consonants – especially at the end of lines."

As the hymn drew to a close, Mr Berry glanced at his watch: 9.25.

Mr Crobert bowed his head and hunched his shoulders and the school followed suit. Mr Crobert asked God to be in various parts of him, listing them in some detail to simplify the Almighty's work. In his eyes and in his seeing. In his head and in his understanding. The school said a reluctant *Amen*.

"Our Father," said Mr Crobert.

"Which art in heaven," said the school.

After prayers, Mr Crobert read out notices. A meeting of the chess club would take place tonight in the gym. Anyone interested in forming a music society should go to Room 16 at

81

four o'clock. That meant, of course, that chess club members interested in forming a music society would have great difficulty. Were there any boys in that predicament? Three hands showed there were. Would they like to give their names to Mr Haynes (Technical Drawing) at dinner time?

The school first team were playing Hartley Tech tomorrow morning and it was hoped as many boys as possible would come along to cheer. Any player picked who did not turn up or arrived without any item of his kit would go straight on the detention list. The names of boys already in detention were read out and Kitchener's name was added.

Mr Berry's watch said: 9.37.

Mr Crobert then turned his attention to the trophy leaning against the side of the lectern. He held it high, displayed it to the back rows and replaced it unsteadily. It was a large ornate silver cup, not unlike the Jules Remy trophy which the England team had won only a year ago. The stem was in the form of a Greek goddess, or some other well-endowed young lady in the habit of wearing curtains, her arms spread out crucifixion-style above her to hold the cup and her feet implanted in a polished wood base made by last year's O level handicraft boys.

"And now," Mr Crobert announced, "the award for best attendance. Four-A came top again last week with 97.3 per cent, but we've disallowed them as they've won three times this term already."

An exaggerated howl of protest rose from 4A.

"Therefore, as a special encouragement, we are awarding the cup to the runners-up – 3B with a very creditable 94 per cent!"

A mild burst of applause followed, mostly from the masters. Surprised at the sudden attention, 3B grinned at each other and fidgeted.

"Had it not been for the illness of Frith – who is now back with us and seems well recovered from his sudden cold – 3A might very well have equalled this figure."

As the stalwarts of 3A rounded on the luckless Frith with hostile looks and whispered threats, Mr Berry again glanced at his watch. It was 9.42. It should, he calculated, take another five minutes for Mr Crobert to wind up, Mr Duckworth to find and play the filing-out-in-order music and the boys to get back to their classrooms and collect their pens and exercise books, so then it would be almost 9.50. He could allow himself three minutes to get to the annexe where 3X would be waiting for him. So he had lost at least 15 minutes from the 40-minute period. Not bad, he thought.

"WALTER SCOTT," Mr Crobert had said to him, "You'll find the boys like that. Boys of their age, full of the stuff of adventure. *Guy Mannering* by Sir Walter Scott."

The boys were now filing out to the strains of Handel's *Hail the Conquering Hero* which grew slower as their lines converged in front of the exits. As 2B marched away with Mr Berry tagging on, Mr Crobert stepped down and placed himself assuredly between the junior master and the door.

"I couldn't help noticing, Berry," he said, "that you were late again this morning. Perhaps I might have a word with you at dinner time." And – with a swirl of gown and a clutching of books – he was gone, out into the corridor and off to his room for the promised encounter with Kitchener.

Mr Berry sighed. He suddenly remembered he still had Dawson's hymn book, but the boy was gone. He would have to give it back later.

THREE-X WERE playing football with a cap when Mr Berry arrived. He shouted at them to sit down, then hit out wildly at three of the boys when they ignored him. His blows failed to land, but the footballers scattered and ran for their seats and the noise diminished a little.

Mr Berry attempted to wipe chalk dust off the master's desk with the same hand but only succeeded in smudging it. It had been very carefully put on with the blackboard wiper which had now disappeared. The desk itself had been moved to the edge of the dais and was in immediate danger of falling off. He pushed it to a safer position and looked round for his chair. It was on the other side of the room, wedged between the stationery cupboard and a window.

"Right!" he said angrily.

"Right!" mimicked the class.

"Jones!" Mr Berry called to the boy nearest the window, "Get my chair out of there!"

There was an expectant silence as Jones left his seat and proceeded to wrestle with the chair. He failed to budge it and howls of laughter went up from the back of the class.

"Are you playing the fool, Jones?"

"No, sir."

"Don't stand for it, sir!" someone yelled. There was another burst of laughter, louder, shriller and more widespread than the previous one. Two boys were rolling round on desktops, clutching their sides as though in pain.

Mr Berry could see that Jones was having genuine difficulty. One arm of the chair had wedged behind a radiator.

"Allright, Jones — sit down." Mr Berry went across to the chair and grappled with it. To loud cheers, he pried it loose and carried it to the dais.

"Right — let's have some quiet!" he bellowed, turning back to the class.

"RIGHT!" yelled the class and the noise swelled.

"Allsop!" Mr Berry waved the boy to come to him and gave him a key. "Allsop, go down to the stockroom. The one by the woodwork room, not the old one upstairs. You'll see a pile of books — *Guy Mannering*, the one we were reading last time. Remember?"

"Yes, sir."

"Right. Bring all the copies you can find. You'll need some help so take someone with you."

"Me, sir!" said Jones who, to Mr Berry's surprise, was still standing where the chair had been wedged.

"Right," said Mr Berry.

"No! Me, sir!" It was Kitchener, bouncing up and down in the second row, obviously fully recovered from his appointment with Mr Crobert, his arm stretched high in the air.

"Please, sir, let me take Kitchener," pleaded Allsop.

"Right. Take both of them. You've got the key. Hurry back."

The three boys galloped away and Mr Berry turned his attention to the class once more. A recurrence of football had broken out at the back. Boys shoved and desks skidded.

"Lewis!" Mr Berry picked on the player who at that moment had possession. "Bring it here – whatever it is you're kicking around! At once! The rest of you sit down!"

Lewis brought the cap to the front of the class. Grumbling loudly, the others sat down.

"And put those desks straight. Quietly."

The desks screeched back into line.

"I said: QUIETLY!" Mr Berry turned his attention to Lewis. "Whose cap is this?"

"I don't know, sir."

"It's not yours?"

"No, sir." Lewis looked startled at the suggestion.

"Is there a name inside? I thought it was a school rule that all caps should have names in."

"Yes, sir. There *is* a name in it, sir."

"Well, what is it?"

Lewis opened the cap, which was torn and dusty. Deep lines fretted his brow as he studied the name.

"Well?"

"I can't read it, sir."

"He can't read it!" shouted the class, delighted. It was an even better joke than when Jones had wrestled with the chair.

"Right!" yelled Mr Berry, "I have had enough of this stupid behaviour! NOW BE QUIET!" He banged his fist on the nearest desk.

The laughter died a little as the front rows considered their vulnerability.

"Give me the cap, Lewis." Mr Berry took the cap. The school badge, he noticed, was hanging by a couple of threads. "Is this the way you treat other people's property, Lewis? You wouldn't do this to your *own* cap!" Mr Berry read the name with difficulty because the ink on the tape was smudged. "Davis," he said to a boy in the third row, "Is this your cap?"

Davis blinked through wire spectacles. "I don't think so, sir."

"What do you mean you don't think so? Is it or isn't it?"

"No, sir."

"Come here, Davis." Davis came. "It's got your name in it. How can you say it isn't yours?"

"Please sir − it isn't." Davis fished in his blazer pocket. "This one is mine."

Mr Berry looked hard at Davis's cap, then back at the cap in his own hand. "Then whose is this?'

Davis thought for a moment. "It could be Davis 3A, sir."

"Yes," said Mr Berry, defeated, "I suppose it could."

"Shall I go and ask him, sir? Three-A are having gym now."

"No, Davis. I'll take care of it later. As for you, Lewis − the next time I catch you kicking other people's property about, I'll put you in detention."

"You don't give the stick to people, do you, sir?" Lewis asked slyly.

"I haven't so far, but don't count on it. Now sit down, the both of you."

As they obeyed, Mr Berry dropped the cap on his desk then turned to face the class once more. "Right..." he began.

"RIGHT!" yelled the class.

Infuriated, Mr Berry picked up the blackboard ruler and stalked along the rows of desks. Immediately there was silence. The blackboard ruler was a yard long and four inches wide. The wood was already cracked from being used as a cane by other masters.

"We have already wasted half this period," shouted Mr Berry, "Now I am simply not going to put up with this any more. I *will* have silence if it means making you sit with your hands on your heads like little babies. In fact, I think that's a good idea. If you won't act like sensible boys, you won't be treated as such."

The boys considered. They believed, in their hearts, that he would never use the blackboard ruler. But they lived in the age of deterrent and the sight of it reminded them that even Mr Berry could be pushed too far. They opted for caution and sat with hands on heads for five or six minutes before spasmodic talking broke out. By this time, Mr Berry had realised that Allsop, Kitchener and Jones were taking far too long fetching the books. He hoped they would return before this fact dawned on the class.

Mercifully, they did. Allsop was in the lead; Kitchener and Jones followed with piles of brown-paper-covered volumes. Allsop fairly beamed. "Where do you want them, sir?"

"On the desk. Just drop them on my desk."

"Can we give them out, sir?"

"Wait a moment," Mr Berry made a quick count. Twenty-five. "Right. Give them out row by row. Some people will have to share, I'm afraid."

"I don't mind sharing, sir."

"That's extremely good of you, Lewis."

"I don't mind not reading it at all, sir." Renewed laughter.

"Sir, is it the one we had last time?"

"That's right, Kitchener."

"I thought it was. Why do we have to read that one, sir? I don't like it."

Mr Berry hesitated. "Well, *some* people like it. It's a very good book."

"*I* don't like it, sir," said somebody at the back and the chant was repeated half a dozen times.

"Please, sir – can we take a vote on who likes it?"

"No. I told you – we've wasted enough time already."

What was left of the period went fairly well. Mr Berry picked the two best readers, two boys who could usually be relied on to take things seriously and make an effort, and the others were tolerably quiet if unattentive. When the bell rang, he had them pass the books to the front before he let them go. They raced for the door. Too late he realised that he would need help to get the books back to the stockroom and that Allsop still had the key.

IT WAS Mr Berry's free period. He sat in the common room with Mr Galvin (PE). The common room was a bleak rectangle surrounded by battered easy chairs, with a few copies of *Punch*, *Time and Tide* and the *New Statesman* lying next to piles of unmarked exercise books. In one corner was a three-bar electric fire, but only one bar worked. Mr Berry and Mr Galvin sat as close to the fire as they dared, warming their splayed hands and trying to ignore their increasingly scorched legs.

"Bloody typical," said Mr Galvin. He was a huge, amiable man with black cropped hair, a full beard and eyebrows that drew a single matted line across the width of his forehead. Despite his easy-going manner with his colleagues, he was known as a strict disciplinarian in the classroom. As well as being in charge of games, Mr Galvin was form teacher of 5X. The fifth forms were the most difficult classes in the school because it was their last year at the old grind and they were eager to get out and start earning money. But 5X were the worst of the worst because they were the positive rejects and had been at the bottom of the pile all their school lives. It was far too late for them to learn anything even if they had once been able to. Mr Galvin was tough, but he wasn't vindictive, and he was genuinely popular with the boys. More popular than I am, thought Mr Berry, even if I *don't* give the stick.

"How you finding it, then?" Mr Galvin was asking, "Teaching, I mean?"

Mr Berry gazed at the single bar and thought about it. It was the question he always dreaded, the question for which he had rehearsed numerous answers, none of them convincing. Sometimes he made a point of looking serious and saying that he thought he was getting the hang of it. Sometimes he allowed himself to show resentment at the question and its obvious implications and was inclined to say "Piece of cake. I wish I'd found out about it sooner." This time he could not make up his mind which course he should take. "It's OK, I guess... not what I expected," he finished lamely.

"You've got no training, of course? No Dip Ed or anything?"

"No. Got my degree and thought I'd see what teaching was all about. See if I liked it." Let's face it, he thought, I'm here because I have no idea how to get what I want in life and I thought I had a future with Sheila Heptinstall.

Memories of the Heptinstall saga made him clench both fists, pressing his fingernails into his palms. When he had been an impoverished undergraduate at Leeds University, reading TS Eliot and wearing his hair like Brian Jones, Sheila Heptinstall had made no secret of her preference for solid, sports-coat-wearing men of a money-earning disposition. So he had given up his dream of hitching down to London to live in a squat and write non-rhyming verse, and had decided to seek lodgings within a bus ride of La Heptinstall and get a steady job with a future. Too late he had discovered that her marked revulsion to all things bohemian, to which he had always credited his lack of progress with her, had in reality masked an overwhelming indifference to him personally. Now here he was in a miserable teaching job in the backwoods of Yorkshire while she, after graduation, had run away to smoke pot in a commune in Muswell Hill and share a bathroom with the road manager of a rock group that had twice been fined for possession of LSD-coated sugar cubes.

"Well, it's not a bad life," Mr Galvin was saying. He laughed. "Folk round here are basically allright. But they don't ask for much, that's the trouble. Life's like mother's milk, they just take it all in. So they grow up, they get a job down the pit, they get the girl next door pregnant and go and live in a Coal Board house. They get up early in the morning and ride to work on a Coal Board bus. They get home at night and watch Z Cars on the telly and go down to the miners' club for four or five pints. We can't teach 'em how to fix themselves a shift on a dry seam or how to suck up to the foreman so they can do a spot of overtime. The kids know that and they get pissed off with us. The best advice I can give you is forget all that educational psychology crap. If a kid steps out of line, hit 'im in the gut." He punched his palm by way of illustration and laughed again.

Mr Berry was reminded of a classic example of the Galvin style: when Bolsover 4X had been suspended for hitting Mr Layden (Chemistry) and had chanced to run into Mr Galvin in the playground as the latter arrived back from a visit to the dentist. What followed had already become legend.

"Ay up, Bolsover," Mr Galvin had said, "What're you doin' out of school, lad?"

"I've been suspended," said a grinning Bolsover.

"Oh," said a politely interested Mr Galvin, "and why've you been suspended, lad?"

"Because I hit Mr Layden," said Bolsover, his grin swelling to unsightly proportions.

At that point, Mr Galvin punched Bolsover on the nose, causing him to sit down heavily on the tarmac. "Well," said Mr Galvin, "I don't suppose you'll be doing that again."

The thing that had most impressed Mr Berry about this particular tale – told to him, perhaps as instruction, on his first day at the school – was not the outright violence of Mr Galvin's response so much as the fact that he had got away with it. Not only had the appalling Bolsover and the equally appalling parents of Bolsover (it was well known his father had several convictions for petty theft and drunkenness) made no attempt to bring the wrath of the law down upon Mr Galvin and the school, but Bolsover, upon his return, had become – if not exactly a model pupil – at least one who conscientiously refrained from hitting teachers. He had eventually gained two O-levels (woodwork and art) and had returned for prize-giving and was last seen shaking Mr Galvin's hand. It was, by any yardstick, a triumph for education.

Mr Berry sighed. He had always shied away from corporal punishment – unless the badly aimed swipes at rowdy pupils which regularly punctuated his lessons, and equally regularly failed to connect – could be described as such. His rationale for this was humanitarian: it was against his principles to use ritual violence against youngsters who, though boisterous, were, he felt, in need of reasoned guidance rather than chastisement.

After all, he asked himself, what sort of example did the violence of adults provide for these youngsters? But nagging doubts assailed him now and then. The obvious characteristic of the Galvin approach was that it got results.

"Bloody typical," repeated Mr Galvin, and Mr Berry assumed their conversation had returned to the question of the lack of civilised heating in the common room. He made no effort to rejoin the talk; he was already thinking about the period after break, with the special reading group from 1C. This consisted of four 11-year-old boys with an average reading age of five-and-a-half. Mr Berry was unsure what he would do with them today.

Perhaps he would get them to make out another set of word cards.

The bell rang for break and Mrs Matthews, the school secretary, came in with a pot of coffee which had been made as usual with hot milk and which Mr Berry always found undrinkable. Mr Galvin rushed to pour some out and rushed back to his seat before the other masters arrived. After that, the others came in, singly or in groups. They discussed the weather, the syllabus, where the key to the gym was. Mr Berry remained silent. Mr Warren (Science) had lost his duplicated diagram of the nitrogen cycle and this meant postponing his planned lesson with 4A. He would have to give them a test on valencies instead. How very annoying. And what fool had left all those damn books on the table? Something by Walter bloody Scott. Mr Bateson again predicted snow for the weekend and the talk turned to sporting fixtures. Would the school football team beat Hartley Tech? Mr Galvin was confident.

"We've got a tough little team. As long as Woodley doesn't get sent off, we'll be OK. And I don't think it's going to snow this side of bloody Christmas."

MR BERRY found the 1C reading group in the library awaiting his arrival. They were playing shove ha'penny on the polished tables but stopped when he entered and pocketed their ha'pennies with guilty grins. All except Crawford, who dared one final shot and scrabbled after it as it bounced on the floor.

"Hello, sir."

"Good morning, Mr Berry sir."

"Good morning, sir."

They were genuinely pleased to see him. Being virtually unable to read meant they missed double geography with the rest of 1C so they could receive his special attention. Also, they liked the library with its potted plants and shiny book jackets. They were, Mr Berry knew, fascinated by books as objects, by their binding and their decoration; all the more so because the words inside remained a mystery.

He had been taking them as a group four times a week since the beginning of term when he and they had first arrived at the school and immediately they had been discovered to be unfit for even the most elementary lessons. But what to do with them in the long-term had not been finalised.

The ideal answer for Crawford, now eagerly gathering chairs for the group, was generally agreed: he was ESN and would have gone to a special school if there had been one in the district. He was a brash, friendly boy with a runny nose and trailing shoelaces, and he lost things – ruler, pencil, exercise book – every three or four minutes. He always had some preposterous excuse for not doing his homework or forgetting his cap and he was passionate in his need to be believed. He was always the first with his hand up, the first to shout out an answer – and he was always wrong. Words were a mere ritual for him, a pattern of delirious activity devoid of meaning. The energy that other boys might spend in thought escaped from Crawford through the constant tapping of his heels and fingers, the twitching of his mouth and nodding of his head.

But the rest were more complex and provided no cut-and-dried solutions: Sullivan was a dull, fawning boy, the temperamental opposite of Crawford. He carried a bright new satchel wherever he went and was always wiping his huge glasses with a spotless handkerchief. He was often absent with colds, even more often bringing a note from his mother to be excused games; and he seemed quite without the desire to do *anything*.

Poynter, a dark quiet boy, was a particular annoyance to Mr Berry. Poynter seemed dull – as dull, God knows, as Sullivan – most of the time; but occasionally he would spring a surprise with a sudden pat answer or a pointed comment that seemed completely out of character, older than his years. Sometimes Mr Berry actually thought Poynter might be laughing at him.

But the one who really interested Mr Berry – the one he guiltily thought of as his favourite – was Partridge. Partridge was a slender boy with blond hair and blue eyes and the angelic appearance that these characteristics readily bestow. He was bright and happy overall; gentle and well-mannered; quick to notice things and able to talk intelligently. But with the written word, it seemed, a curtain came down in his mind: he could not relate the symbols on the page to the sounds that he uttered.

When the group was seated round him, Mr Berry handed out sheets of paper. There were horrified cries of "Test!" and gasps and exaggerated groans.

"That's right. It's a test,'" said Mr Berry. He had decided, in the end, to follow the example of Mr Warren. "It's a test on the days of the week. You've been learning them for the last two homeworks. But just to get you word perfect, I'll give you five minutes to look them up in your word books."

"Please, sir, please... Somebody's stolen my book, sir."

"You mean you left it at home, Crawford. Share with Partridge."

For the next six or seven minutes, there was only muttering and grimacing as the boys set to, memorising the shapes which they had all copied down into their books the week before.

"Right," said Mr Berry, "Close your books. Stop singing, Crawford! The test is about to begin. Write your names on the papers so we don't get them all mixed up. Right. Number one. First day of the week: Sunday."

Pencils scratched. Mr Berry had already discovered that pens were too sophisticated for certain members of the group and only led to hold-ups. "Goodo, sir, I know that one," said Crawford.

"Good for you, Crawford."

"He doesn't know it really, does he, sir?"

"We'll see when it's over, Poynter. Next: Wednesday. That's a hard one."

"Please, sir, Partridge is looking at my paper."

"I am *not!*"

"Well, don't let him, Crawford. Cover the answer with your hand. Next: Friday."

"Wait a minute, sir. You're going too fast!"

"Allright, Sullivan, I'll give you chance to catch up." Mr Berry counted to 57 in his head. "Thursday."

"What was the one before, sir?"

"Wednesday, Crawford."

"No, sir, I mean the one before that."

"I'll go over them again. Number one was Sunday, number two was Friday, number three was Wednesday, number four is Thursday."

"Do we have to number them, sir? You didn't say we had to number them."

Mr Berry sighed. "You're right, Poynter, I didn't. Yes, please, number them down the left hand side. It's my fault. I should have told you. I'll wait for you to do it."

Number five was Tuesday, number six Monday and number seven Saturday.

"Just like it is in real life," said Poynter, "Saturday is the seventh day, sir."

Was there a mocking tone in Poynter's voice? Mr Berry could not be sure. "And just to make the number up to ten," he said, a trifle needled, "we'll make the last three the names of months."

This time there were cries of genuine indignation. "You didn't give us those for homework, sir."

"Yes I did, Sullivan. I gave you three homeworks on names of months and when I gave you a test, you all did so badly that I decided I'd have to test you again."

"Oh, sir..." Partridge's cry petered out into something like despair.

"I don't mind," said Crawford, "I like the months better than the days."

Number eight was June, number nine January and number ten May. The test was over.

Crawford clicked his fingers, moaned and stamped his feet as he scanned his work; Partridge gazed into empty space for last-minute inspiration, then pushed his paper away resignedly; Sullivan was glancing slyly over to where Mr Berry had written the answers on his own piece of paper; Poynter put a cough sweet in his mouth and sucked noisily, ignoring library rules about sweets and noise.

Mr Berry picked up the papers and leafed through them. Crawford, as usual, seemed to be employing his own alphabet; Poynter got his usual six out of ten; Sullivan had got four right – and it might have been five if his writing had not suddenly plunged into the unintelligible. Partridge had given only two answers: one might have been a stab at *January* except that it was the number where *Friday* should have been. The other word was: *suntdot*.

"Well, that was pretty bad. You two – Partridge and Crawford – get nought. But *none* of you have any reason to be pleased." Sullivan stopped giggling as Mr Berry shot him a glance of annoyance. "Now, let's have another look at the days. They're not as hard as all that..." Mr Berry tried to make his tone convincing.

The boys all opened their word books, except Crawford who pushed up against Partridge.

"In the first place," said Mr Berry, "let me give you a tip: all the days of the week have the same ending. What is it?"

The group looked blank.

"Well, it's *day*, isn't it? They all end in *day*. I'm sure I've said this before. If you know how to spell *day*, you've just got to fit the first part of the word on to it. So you've got half the word already."

"'Not with Saturday," said Poynter, looking shrewd, "Saturday's a very long word."

"And Wednesday's very long too," said Sullivan.

"But they all end in *day*, and some of you don't even know how to spell that." He wrote the word in large letters on a piece of paper and held it up. "Now copy it."

"Shall we copy it in our word books, sir?"

"Of course."

"Please, sir..."

"You can do it on paper, Crawford. Here."

After giving Crawford a piece of paper, he went and looked out of the window at the slag heap on the other side of the playing field. Then, when he felt he had given them enough time, he looked at every wordbook in turn. They had all written something resembling *day*. "Now remember that word – especially Crawford and Partridge. It's very simple."

"I can write it down as long as I'm looking at it," said Partridge, "I'm not good at remembering."

"I can see that from your test. What was that supposed to mean?" Mr Berry pointed to the first answer on the paper.

Partridge's face went blank.

95

"Come on! What day was that supposed to be?"

"Saturday, sir?"

"No, not Saturday. *S, u, n.* What does *that* spell?"

Partridge continued to look blank.

Mr Berry repeated the letters, then said "*s-uuu-nn*" in a very elongated way so that each letter was sounded separately.

"Sun... Sunday!" said Partridge.

"Only half right. Because then you've got a *t* – I think that's a *t* – so that makes *sunt*. And then you've got *d, o, t.*"

He then pronounced both syllables in an elongated way, hoping that Partridge would hear the letters fitting together. "What have you got then, Partridge?"

The boy tightened the corners of his mouth to show he was thinking desperately hard.

"Well, I'll tell you," said Mr Berry, "you've got *suntdot.*"

A look of suspicion crept over Partridge's face.

"And you know what *suntdot* means?"

"No, sir."

"Of course you don't. There's no such word. You've made it up. You've invented a new word."

The look of suspicion faded. Partridge burst out laughing. The others, who were by now fighting over a rubber lying on the floor by Poynter's chair, looked over in amazement.

AT DINNER time, Mr Berry sat at a table with six boys from 2C and ate cheese pie with lettuce and chips followed by semolina with jam in the middle. For the next hour, he sat in the common room reading the *New Statesman*. There was a particularly interesting article on Harold Wilson and the planned economy. The sun had come out at midday and the common room was warm enough for masters to sit as far away from the fire as they wanted. At a quarter to two, they even turned off the remaining bar. In the secretary's room next door, the radio was playing *What a Wonderful World*. Against this background, Mr Berry fell asleep.

And so he forgot he had to see Mr Crobert.

AFTERWARDS, MR Berry went to his lesson with the whole of 1C, who were the class he knew best. Apart from special sessions with the reading group, he took the full class of 35 boys five times a week for an assortment of lessons under the umbrella titles of English, History and Religious Instruction.

English with 1C meant getting them to put verbs into sentences and making their writing legible; History was drawing caves and stone axes; Religion meant maps of the Holy Land and the Red Sea in crayon.

Their classroom was the annexe in the playground. It was cold again now because the radiators didn't work and some of the boys sat with their coats on. The annexe was actually a chemistry lab. There were gas taps on the benches and sinks with running water and the room had the bad egg smell of all such places.

When they saw Mr Berry, the whole class broke into a ragged cheer. He opened his briefcase onto his desk and waited for the noise to subside. "Right," he said, "you have two pieces of work to show me by the end of the period..."

"Please, sir, can I leave the room?"

"Allright, Keeley. But you should have gone during break. And hurry back."

"Can I go too, sir?"

"Wait until Keeley gets back, McLean. I'm not having troops of boys leaving my lesson."

"But, sir..."

"No. Now, the two things I want...."

"Please, sir, is it History?"

"No, McLean. History is on Monday. We're doing RI now. Two things: you have to draw those pictures in your scripture book – I'll give the books out in a minute – and copy out the chapter headed *Palestine Under the Romans* that I went over with you last Tuesday."

He wrote his instructions on the blackboard with the title of the book, the chapter heading and the page numbers.

"Please, sir, I've finished all those."

"All of them, Tucker?" The pictures were: a Roman soldier, a Pharisee, a Jewish temple or Synagogue, and a Fishing

Boat of the Kind Used on the Sea of Galilee at the Time of Our Lord.

"Yes, sir."

"And you've copied out the chapter?"

"Well, almost, sir."

"Right. Finish the chapter and bring it to me to mark. And don't rush so I can't read your writing. Bring it to me only when you're sure you've finished. Henderson! If I catch you turning on the gas again, I'll smack your head. It's a stupid, dangerous thing to do."

"Please sir – Crawford turned on the water tap."

Crawford quickly turned it off and leapt back.

"Is that stupid and dangerous too, sir?" demanded Henderson.

"No. Just stupid. And Crawford will get his head smacked if he does it again." Mr Berry unlocked the text book cupboard in the corner of the lab and gave a pile of *The Life and Work of Jesus* to the nearest boy on each bench. They passed them round noisily and took out their exercise books. There were the usual problems: three boys without exercise books, one without a satchel altogether, and Crawford without anything.

"I'll lend you my own pen, Crawford, and you can share crayons with Jackson."

"But, sir – somebody *stole* my pencils. Somebody stole them."

"It's a serious thing to accuse people of stealing, Crawford. Have a good look round at home tonight."

"Sir," Sullivan called out, "When are we having you for reading again, sir?"

"I'll be seeing the reading group last period this afternoon."

"Oh, that's good, sir!' yelled Crawford, jumping up and down in anticipation.

Suddenly the hubbub died. Mr Berry looked round involuntarily. Mr Crobert was already in the room. "Crawford," he called, "come here!"

Crawford slunk unwillingly to the front of the class.

"The last time I saw you, Crawford," Mr Crobert beamed and placed a hand on Crawford's head, "I told you to get your shoelaces tied. Did you remember to do it?"

Crawford gulped. "Yes, sir."

Mr Crobert looked down at Crawford's feet. The laces were tied tightly and neatly. Mr Crobert took his hand off Crawford's head and gave him a sharp smack across the face.

Crawford stepped back sharply. His eyes filled with tears.

"Do you know what that was for, Crawford?"

"No, sir," said a weeping Crawford.

"You've remembered once, and that's all very well. The smack was to make sure you remember *every* time."

The class giggled awkwardly, knowing that Mr Crobert had scored a point but suspicious that he had cheated. The headmaster motioned Crawford back to his seat.

"Mr Berry, I'd like a word with you in my office."

"Yes, Mr Crobert."

"You boys, I'm sure, have work to be getting on with. No noise now. Or I shall be back to crack a few more heads."

In a moment, he was gone. Mr Berry followed.

MR CROBERT'S office wall was a gallery of Croberts. A youthful Crobert in cap and gown clutching his diploma glowered from an ornate silver frame. He peered from the left side of a second row of masters in a panoramic school photograph of, guessed Mr Berry, some 20 years ago. He appeared at subsequent points in his life in cricket flannels or football shirt, in raincoat and trilby, in anorak and wellingtons. He stood alongside the mayor at prize-giving and sat next to the chairman of the PTA at the annual parents' day. Finally, he gazed out resolutely from the middle of the front row of the Drivers Lane staff photograph of two summers ago, the year when he had been promoted to headmaster – the captain and centre forward of the teaching team.

The bookshelf behind the desk had a Bible, the *Shorter Oxford*, *Wind in the Willows* and *Quentin Durward*. The Schools' League football trophy for the previous year hung above the medal won by Shaw 4X for representing Yorkshire at swimming.

Mr Crobert sat at his desk, the desktop empty except for a huge square of pristine blotting paper and a gardener's calendar. Mr Berry pulled up the wooden chair on the near side and pushed the door shut with his elbow. The headmaster took his time lighting his pipe. Finally, he said: "I can't help but notice, Mr Berry, that you've been late several times in the past fortnight. Is there any special reason for this?"

"No. Not really."

"Well, I'm sure you'll make a greater effort in future. Let me see – it's almost a whole term since you came to us. I hope you're settling in allright."

A pause.

"Yes," said Mr Berry.

"And I hope you've found that teaching is the career for you."

Another pause.

After a while, Mr Crobert said: "It's a very exacting profession, of course. Not just a matter of imparting facts, as you will have found already. Teaching means enforcing discipline, commanding respect and setting a constant example. What are we here for, after all? We're here to mould useful citizens. Oh, I know we don't get the cream at Drivers Lane. No, some people would say we have the rejects." He allowed himself an ironic smile.

"But I look at it this way: it's a challenge. We've got to show these boys there's more in life than long-haired pop groups and a night at the pub. We've got to set standards, for them and ourselves. That's why we make sure they clean their shoes and get their hair cut. All part of our job; much more so if their parents won't do it. The reason I encourage so much sport at Drivers Lane," he waved a hand at the football trophy, "is to give the boys something to be proud of. It's all part of the same thing – a sense of duty to society, in this case to the school.

"You see what I'm getting at? And you see now why I'm keen that all my masters get in on time? Why I'm so strict about that sort of thing? We must set an example. And there are other ways in which you can help, Mr Berry. Extracurricular activities play an important part in school life. *Any* school. When Mr Parkin leaves at the end of term, there'll be nobody to organise the cross-country club. I was thinking... perhaps you'd like to take it over?"

There was another pause.

Then: "Yes," Mr Berry heard himself say.

"Good. There are some young people today who mock the very idea of civic duty, of team spirit. But I'm glad to see that you and I are in broad agreement."

His pipe had gone out. He re-lit it and looked at his watch. "I'm also glad we had this little heart-to-heart. I must attend to some other matter now, but I'll tell Mr Parkin about your offer. I'm sure it will be a great relief to him to know that his work will go on."

WHEN MR Berry returned to the annexe, the class had already gone. He put away the textbooks left lying in heaps, turned off three gas taps and opened the windows. Later, in the common room, he tried to mark 2B's English books, due back on Monday. But he found he couldn't concentrate.

One more period, he thought to himself, and it would be the weekend. The 1C reading group again – and he had nothing prepared.

The perfect strategy for the unprepared lesson had been explained to him in his first week, long before he had heard it reiterated by the likes of Mr Warren. The *test* meant at least ten minutes to give out papers and get them to write their names, ten questions at two minutes a question, and ten minutes for marking. And if you mistimed it, you could always spend another ten minutes taking in the marks. But, of course, he had already given them one test today.

Perhaps they could return to the days of the week. Or he could start labelling objects again, as he had done some weeks ago... *table, chair, window, door...*

When he reached the library, it was already occupied by some fifth formers in their revision period. In fact, they were playing cards and it was too late for them to hide the fact when he walked in. The cards didn't really bother Mr Berry, though it was breaking school rules. But the noise did. He moved the players to the far end of the room, behind some shelves, and told them to keep quiet. By now, the reading group had arrived. They dragged some chairs round the nearest table and gazed at him expectantly.

"Now, remember this morning? Remember what we did?"

Their expressions were as blank as always.

"The days of the week. Remember?"

They nodded. Poynter said: "I got six out of ten, didn't I, sir?"

"Oh sir! I bet I could get ten out of ten if we had it now sir!"

"Do you want another test then?"

There were cries of "Shurrup, Crawford!" and moans and kicks under the table.

"Allright. No more tests."

Gasps of relief.

"We're going to..." Mr Berry thought hard. "We're going to *think* for this period. We're going to think about... a *composition*. We won't write anything. Not today, at least. We're just going to think about it.

"First, we've got to have a subject. Something we want to write about. What do *you* want to write about, Sullivan?"

Sullivan blinked. The question, his expression seemed to say, was distinctly unfair, coming out of the blue as it had. He wrinkled his face in concern, then looked at his feet. Finally, he took off his glasses and put them on again.

"Come on, Sullivan, what is the thing that interests you most of all? What do you *really* like doing?" Mr Berry would have thought twice before asking 3X, or anyone older than 1C, that sort of question. But with his reading group, he felt safe.

"Train numbers, sir."

"You like to go train-spotting?"

"Yes, sir."

"Oh, sir! Sir!" Crawford was waving his hand. "Football, sir! I like football!"

"Which team do you support, sir?" asked Poynter, "Leeds?"

"It doesn't matter which team I support, Poynter."

"Sir supports Barnsley, don't you, sir?" said Partridge. Mr Berry remembered having told him once about watching Barnsley play.

"Barnsley's no good, sir."

"Better than rotten old Leeds. Better than..."

"Right," said Mr Berry, heading off trouble, "Right, Crawford. You want to write about football?"

"Yes, please sir." Crawford jogged up and down, waving his arms and snapping his fingers. He was in his element and scored a goal left-footed against the table leg.

"Football's no good," it was Partridge again, showing his independence, "I'm going to write about fishing."

"You go fishing?"

"Yes, sir. Me and my dad. Sometimes we go to the Addlethorpe Dam. Fishing's better than football. Last month my dad caught a..." he struggled for the name, "I think it was a perch, sir. Something like that. *I* didn't catch anything though," he ended apologetically.

"What shall *I* write about, sir?" asked Poynter.

"I don't know. What do you *want* to write about?"

"Nothing, sir."

The others were convulsed with laughter. "That's good, sir. You did *ask* him! Let him write about nothing." It had not occurred to any of them yet that they could, in fact, write little more than their names; and, in Poynter's case, six days of the week.

Mr Berry silenced them with an upraised hand. "Come on, Poynter. There must be something you've done recently that you'd like to tell us about. Something you did at home..."

Poynter considered. Finally: "We moved house last week, sir."

"That's very interesting. Why don't you write about that?"

"It's *not* interesting, sir. It's boring."

"When did you move?"

"Last week, sir. Thursday."

"You remember, sir," said Partridge, "Last Thursday when Poynter wasn't here.'" Only he said the word *firsday*.

"I'm going to write about Bobby Charlton, sir. I saw him on the telly. Not going to write about rotten old Barnsley," said Crawford.

"Last *firsday*," said Partridge.

"Thursday," said Mr Berry.

"That's what I said, sir."

"Train numbers is very interesting, sir." Sullivan obviously felt left out.

Mr Berry raised his voice and they were quiet, but the resulting silence at the table threw into relief the noise from the far end of the room. Mr Berry went across to warn the card players. When he came back, he said to Partridge: "Not *firsday* but *Thursday*. Say it like this." He said it very deliberately, tapping his tongue against his front teeth.

"*Firsday*," said Partridge.

"No. *Th*, not *f!*" Mr Berry pronounced both sounds distinctly. 'Not *form* or *Friday*. Thursday."

"Firsday."

"Thursday."

"Firsday."

"Look..." Mr Berry was beginning to lose patience. "*Thurs*day, right? Can't you hear the difference?"

"No, sir."

"Of course you can."

"No I can't, sir. I'm deaf." Partridge squirmed in his seat.

"Don't be silly. You can hear me now."

"Just about, sir. Sometimes I can hear allright if your lips move a lot."

Mr Berry hesitated. Was he being made a fool of? If the revelation had come from Poynter, he would have been certain of trickery. If it had come from Crawford... "Are you serious, Partridge? How long have you been like this?"

Partridge, suddenly the centre of attention, looked round uneasily at the others. "I don't know, sir."

"Why didn't you tell me before?"

"I don't know, sir."

"You're not making this up?"

Partridge was outraged. "Oh no, sir!"

"Why haven't you told anybody else? What about your parents?"

Partridge squirmed again. "I did, sir. I told my dad. He said I was just being stupid."

The room seemed to spin in front of Mr Berry's eyes. He clutched the edge of the table.

"Are we going to do our writing now, sir?" said Poynter, "because I still don't know what to write about."

The room had come to rest and Mr Berry let go of the table. "No," he said, "no, we won't." He took a sheaf of paper out of his briefcase. "Here. Take one of these each."

"Oh, sir, not a test! You said..."

"I know what I said. I've changed my mind, Poynter. That's what comes of not being able to think of anything to write about."

Poynter accepted with bad grace, muttering to himself unintelligibly. He and the others took the sheets and laid them on the table.

"Now," said Mr Berry, "I want you to put your name at the top of the paper. You can all do that, can't you?"

They did so with varying degrees of success.

"Right," said Mr Berry, "Now I want you to number one to ten down the left hand side. Like this." He took a sheet and showed them. They did as they were told.

"Now I want you to copy out these words." He wrote next to the numbers: *Monday, Tuesday, Wednesday, Thursday, Friday, Saturday, January, February, suntdot*. He turned the paper round and laid it in front of them so they could all see it. They leaned over the table, puzzled and excited, and copied the words. When everyone except Crawford had finished, Poynter said: "This is very funny, sir. Why are we doing it?"

"It's something to show Mr Crobert. An achievement. An example of... team spirit!"

Poynter looked unconvinced. "What do we do now, sir?"

"I want you all to put a tick next to the answers on numbers one to nine."

They did so. "What about number ten?" asked Poynter.

"Put a cross by that one. That one is wrong."

They looked at Mr Berry, they looked at each other, they shrugged, they smiled, Crawford kicked the table leg. They put their crosses.

Mr Berry collected the papers. "Thank you," he said, "You've worked very hard. We've all worked very hard. *You're* tired. *I'm* tired. We're all looking forward to the weekend."

"Sir," asked Poynter, "Why have we put a wrong answer?"

"Because," said Mr Berry, "perfection is suspect."

MR BERRY went to Mr Crobert's office as soon as the bell rang. He did not show Mr Crobert the papers, but he did report Partridge's statement about being deaf. Mr Crobert checked with the primary school record, but there was no mention of it. "Nevertheless," he said, "I shall pursue the matter first thing on Monday."

"Another thing," said Mr Berry, "I'm afraid you'll need someone else for the cross-country club next term. I've decided teaching isn't for me and I'm resigning. You can have it in writing on Monday morning."

"Well," said Mr Crobert with the closest he ever allowed to surprise. He reached for his pipe. "This is most unexpected. Have you thought about the boys? You have a duty to them, to do what's best."

"Yes," said Mr Berry, "I've thought about the boys. I really have."

ON THE WAY home, he passed two boys fighting and separated them. The bigger one was Dawson 3A. Mr Berry reached into his pocket and found the hymn book.

"Oh, thank you, sir," said Dawson, relieved not to be punished.

"Don't thank me," said Mr Berry, "I'm glad to be rid of it." He looked at the other boy and noticed he was bare-headed. Recognition dawned. "It's Davis, isn't it? Davis 3A?"

"Yes, sir," said the second boy, alarmed.

"I've got something for you, too." Mr Berry rummaged in his briefcase and produced the cap. "I'm even more glad to be rid of *this*."

He looked once more at the boys then up at the glowering sky. Mr Bateson had been right after all. It was starting to snow.

Priceless!

1. Angela

I AM AWAKE. Yes, I must be.

As I walked through the wilderness of this world, I lighted on a certain place and I laid me down in that place to sleep and as I slept I dreamed a dream. And suddenly I dreamed no more and I awoke and it was day.

No, no. I see it is not day. It is light because the ceiling light in my cell is always on. But it is not day.

In Wakefield Prison I had a dream. I dreamed I was in Wakefield Prison. But now I am awake and still I dream.

In my dream I hear these words: "John Garlick Poulson, the magnitude and evil nature of what you have done is such that I have no choice but to sentence you to seven years."

In the beginning is the word. The word told me: John Garlick Poulson, architect of Pontefract, gird up your loins for what you must do. You must write your story. You must write a book. Yes, yes, that is what I must do!

Of course, more than one object is in my mind. First and foremost is the desire to tell my side of the story – my testament of downfall, bankruptcy and imprisonment for corruption – if only to prevent others being trapped in the same plight!

Secondly, I believe I have a debt to my family to reveal truths which have lain in the darkness as I myself now lie in darkness which the light on my ceiling can never fully disperse.

And thirdly, I mean to see my creditors are paid in full from the proceeds of my book. Already they have received well over 50 per cent, and there is only £100,000 left owing. A paltry sum indeed considering the large amounts that I have earned for my country over the years! And it finally gives the lie to those scurrilous newspaper reports about how my debts run to millions. Here at last is the truth. The truth as I remember it. The truth as I know it.

And anyway, what else have I to do? I have nothing much to look forward to. I am almost 70 now and living on borrowed time. I despair at the state of the country. That appalling Harold Wilson has finally gone, but his small-minded party remains in power. And I don't see that Callaghan person doing any better.

Then, said Christian, what means this? The angel explained: A little distance from this gate there is erected a strong castle, of which Satan is the captain. From thence, he and his acolytes shoot arrows at those who come up to this gate, so they may die before they can enter into eternal bliss. Then, said Christian, I do both tremble and rejoice. I do tremble for fear of death and rejoice that the host of the Lord will protect and succour me.

I make no apologies for naming names. The guilty men know their misdeeds and malpractices must be exposed. They are more familiar with wrong-doing than ever I was. Yes, I was guilty. But only of folly, lack of consideration for my own money. For I have laboured hard for my friends and my country. It was the folly of trusting others, people who had every reason to repay my trust. Instead they violated it.

But how to go about it? How to write it? How to start? O Lord, merciful God, I am cast down among mine enemies. I am eyeless in Gaza. Hear, O Lord, my gnashing of teeth. Help me find a way…

And there she was. She carried a portable electric typewriter and a cardboard folder. She put them on my table. She said: "Hello Mr P! It's a cold morning." She held up a flex with a plug at the end. She said: "Where do I plug this in?"

I said: "You can't. We don't have electric points. Not in the cells. They're afraid of suicides."

She said: "Oh dear, then I suppose we'll just have to pretend." And then she picked up a kettle which I'd never seen before and she said: "I'll pretend to make some tea as well."

And she did. And it was just the way I like it. Plenty of milk and lots of sugar.

I said: "Thank you, Miss…Miss…"

"Angela. Angela Record. Miss Long Player if you take my age into account. That's what my friends always say."

"I believe God has sent you."

"Well, if he did, Mr P, he must be running the Right Type Agency on the Dewsbury Road. They said you were writing a book. What's it about then?" She sat on my chair, but that was fine because I was quite comfortable on the bottom bunk.

She opened the cardboard folder, took out a sheet of typing paper and wound it into the machine.

I said: "It's about how my world fell about me. It's about my courtroom ordeal lasting 52 days and 52 nights."

"Oh dear," she sighed, "I can see it's not going to be a lorry-load of laughs then. Not like the usual Yorkshire memoirs. Not like that nice James Herriott and All Vets Great and Small. Still, if it's all a bit down in the dumps, you'll probably tend to speak more slowly. That's always a useful thing in my profession. I'm considered quite fast but I always like to be careful." She laughed. "Just my little joke." She sat, poised to type. "Right, Mr P. Go ahead then."

"Right. But where shall I start?"

"Well, people usually say *begin at the beginning*. But I say it's up to you. Start anywhere you like. The first thing that comes into your head."

"Very well." I threw off the blankets and stood up. I had slept in my prison uniform – a sort of dark blue boiler suit. So I was perfectly decent. I started to pace, which was something I often did in my cell. I said: "A prison bus from Armley Jail took me and George to Leeds Crown Court..."

"George? Who's George?"

"That's George Pottinger, the very distinguished assistant secretary of state for Scotland. Well, he *was* very distinguished. At the time."

"George Pottinger, very distinguished assistant secretary. It's just as well to explain who everybody is as you go along, Mr P."

"Yes, of course. You know, George beat all the other candidates when he passed the Civil Service examination. He then went to war and became one of England's youngest lieutenant colonels. And he pursued a gallant role in the Italian campaign. In 1953, he was honoured by the Queen for arranging her coronation visit to Scotland."

"Ah. Well, I don't think you need *quite* so much detail, Mr P. Not at this point. You can always have an appendix at the end…"

"He has achieved so much in his lifetime! When I first met him, he was in his fifties, but he looked much younger. He was urbane, unruffled, with an outstanding presence. His height is not exceptional, it is true, and there is nothing particularly striking about his dark, well groomed hair and clean Scottish features. What is impressive is his absolutely brilliant mind and flashing wit."

"Flashing wit," she repeated in her very professional way as she typed along.

"That was what immediately attracted me. What can I say of this man I so admired? He hypnotised me. He was manly in every possible way, still fit and trim and playing tennis regularly. I wanted to help him, to give him what was so easy for me. What I did for him seemed only a trifle."

"Yes, well, trifle is as trifle does. I'm sure you know that, Mr P. Let's get back to the court, shall we?"

"I stood in the dock with George beside me. You may find it hard to believe, but we were both equally confident that we would be released. Then the jury, three women and nine men, filed in and took their seats. The foreman rose to his feet."

"Rose to his feet."

"He was a Yorkshireman, perhaps a schoolmaster. I can see them now, the people on the jury. Ordinary little people, the sort of people my father had employed by the hundred in his famous pottery works. All the bickering and badgering, the probing and the questioning, had been far beyond even *my* comprehension, let alone these honest local tradesmen with their limited application. Even so, it was with amazement that I saw the foreman's lips move in answer to that terrible question. The word guilty came astonishingly to my ears."

"To my ears."

"To say I was completely shattered is an understatement. How had this happened to me? What Machiavellian intertwining of malicious circumstance had led me to this impossible infamy? Had I but known it, the way things would turn out, perhaps I would have managed things differently. Perhaps, as I write my story, an answer will emerge."

"Will emerge." She paused. "Right, Mr P. That's very interesting. But I've had another think about it. Now I have to say I think you should start with something a bit more personal."

"Personal? What do you mean?"

"Childhood. You need childhood in an autobiography. Like *David Copperfield*. There's lots of childhood in David Copperfield. And *Oliver Twist*. Though maybe *Oliver Twist* is not the best comparison I should be making. I mean, all that *gotta pick a pocket or two* stuff. Sorry about that. But people like to know that sort of thing. They like to know where people come from. That's how you get to know a person, by knowing where they come from."

"I leave the world to judge me, Miss Record…"

"Angela."

"Angela. Oh very well. Childhood. Well…"

"You did have one, didn't you?"

I said: "Of course." Then I realised it was another joke.

"For instance, how did you get on with your father? Was he a good role model, that sort of thing?"

I told her my father was a wonderful man, that he was mild, generous and firm in his convictions, and he always placed his faith in self-discipline and decent conduct. I never knew him to use violence when it could be avoided, though my brother and I often felt his strap when we refused to obey his commands.

"Commands," said Angela.

I added, of course, that it was my grandfather, one of the greatest men in Yorkshire politics, whom I took for my example in my formative years. He was open-handed and generous to an extreme in a way far more acceptable in *his* day than it was to be in mine. My grandfather was the Justice of the Peace who read the Riot Act to the striking miners in Featherstone. Troops from Pontefract Barracks escorted him. He was also compassionate, of course. We employed 4,000 men at our Ferrybridge works and the wellbeing of the workforce was a source of great pride and strength to him. And every year he sent a sack of coal to every widow in Ferrybridge.

"Widow in Ferrybridge," said Angela, "Lovely."

One thing I noticed when I visited my grandfather was that he often had guests in the house and I saw how relaxed and friendly even the most important people became in his company. Professional men, I realised, were quickly transformed into easy-going human beings by a good meal and a glass of something pleasant. Though I hardly ever drink myself.

I then explained how my ancestors had begun in Staffordshire, but moved to Yorkshire in the 19th century. The difficulty in making good pottery in Yorkshire was that the local folk were not really skilled enough. Not very intelligent. Nevertheless, we persevered.

"Persevered," said Angela, "What about early setbacks then? Struggles against hardship? That sort of thing goes down very well with the general reader. What about your mother?"

"My mother…" I paused because this was indeed hard. "My mother died when I was young. She was an invalid all her life. She suffered terribly from asthma."

I told her one of my earliest memories was of sitting beside my mother's bed. I often read to her from the Bible. You know, my parents were strong Methodists and I myself found the Bible stories inspiring. And one night, I remember, I was reading her the story of the five loaves and two fishes. *And Jesus looked up to heaven and he praised God and he blessed and broke them, the loaves and fishes, and he gave them to the disciples, the faithful twelve, to set before the crowd. And all the great crowd ate of them and were satisfied and cried out that he was truly the Messiah.* And my mother took my hand and said: "John. Always remember the Lord loveth a cheerful giver." And I said: "Yes, mother, yes I will."

A cheerful giver. "It was a maxim I practised throughout my life."

Angela said: "Well, that's parents for you. They never know the trouble they cause. You know what Philip Larkin said about parents, don't you?"

I had to say: "No."

"He said… well, he said they mess you about a lot."

I said: "You'll want to know about my arm."

She said: "Will I?" But then she realised how important it must be. "Fine. Go ahead."

113

I told her how my father was one of the oldest members of the County Cricket Association and in my youth I also had a great love of cricket. But at the age of 12, I developed *osteomyelitis* in my arm.

She asked me how to spell it, but I had to admit I didn't know. She said: "I'll look it up later."

I told her how the surgeon wished to amputate, but my father said: *You will not rob him of his right arm.* "You see. I still have it."

"Yes. I noticed you had two arms as soon as I came in." I believe it was another of her jokes.

I said: "We saved the arm. But my cricketing ambitions were at an end and I was never free from a certain nagging discomfort for the rest of my life." I rubbed my arm to demonstrate. "Still, there's always a silver lining. Those of us who live with pain learn that there are always others worse off than ourselves. And that is what I have told myself many times during my imprisonment."

Then she asked me to talk about my schooldays.

I told her my father had sent me to the Methodist public school where he himself had been educated. But they did not do well for me. The truth is that academic standards had been lowered by the terrible mortality of the Great War. You may find it hard to believe but some of the masters seemed as young as the senior boys, while others were practically senile. When my results showed how badly the school was failing me, my father took me away and had me privately tutored.

So what was to become of me if I could not be a cricketer? My father's plan was this – I should work in a bank. Without qualifications there was not much a boy could do, he believed, except seek the shelter of a decent occupation such as a bank might provide. But I wanted, I suddenly told him, to become an architect. Yes! From the time I was old enough to be permitted my own periodical journal, I had been fascinated by pictures of churches and other splendid exotic buildings. My father was surprised. And, I think, impressed. He agreed. I joined a firm of respected architects renowned for their work on public houses. I myself, of course, was unlikely to see many examples of their work first-hand. My father paid the premium of £250 for my training. I also took a course in drawing at Leeds College of Art and arranged privately to study quantity surveying.

"But you never qualified, did you? Why was that? Were you unhappy?"

I struggled to overcome my annoyance. "Unhappy? No, no! I revelled in the training and those four years passed like wildfire. My father provided me with a car and pocket money and one thing I *did* concentrate on was my appearance. My father always impressed on me the need to be well turned-out."

I then felt this needed more explanation so I added: "It's a sad fact that some people *have* described me as an unqualified architect. They say I failed to complete the course at Leeds College. But I personally do not recognise the word *fail*. No, the reason I started my own business as soon as I did was that one of the college masters recognised my unquenchable enthusiasm. *Go out on your own as soon as you finish your articles*! he advised me.

"Another thing people have said about me is that I was sacked by my employers for getting the elevation of my buildings the wrong way round. No-one who knows me would believe such a thing. No! With sincerity, I have to say I was removed when the company was suddenly taken over by people who did not know how to value me. I'm afraid the world is full of such people and I am not the only man of talent to suffer at their hands. The truth was: I had mastered the rudiments of quantity surveying, so I did not hesitate to take the plunge and start my own company."

"Now," she said, and I'm sorry to say she appeared to giggle, "what about romance? That's another great hook for the readers. Tell me about your love life, Mr P. Don't be shy. There you were, as you say, well turned out, with your motor car and all that pocket money. There had to be young ladies."

"It's true," I said, "I fell in love. In Wales."

She then made some facetious comment about foreign parts which I later realised was quite indecent. And she asked me for details. "They can be quite intimate if you like. We live in an intimate age, don't you think?"

I told her it was not an intimate age in 1936. Far from it. I was 26. I was on holiday. Nine days after our first meeting, I proposed. And she refused me.

"Oh dear," said Angela.

"But only at first. I persisted. In a polite and decorous way, of course."

"Of course."

"And in the end she accepted me."

And we had been happily married ever since, with two charming daughters. Adopted, as it happens. I told how we lived with my father for many years because of the wartime building restrictions. Then in 1957, Harold Macmillan, whom I regard as one of our greatest prime ministers, removed them. So I designed my own house. It won a prize.

I explained how the removal of building restrictions was good news for many of us. Like Dan, for instance. At this, she clicked her tongue and reiterated her previous remark that I had to explain who the people were.

2. Mr Newcastle

I SAID: "T. Dan Smith. Mr Newcastle!"

"You mean he was a body-builder?"

"No, no. Oh, another joke, I see. But he built almost everything else. He was the man who rebuilt Newcastle."

Meeting Dan was a turning point in my life. When I first met him, he held out his hand right away. He said: "*Haway*, John man." This was because he came from Newcastle.

I said: "*Haway*, Dan," because I thought it was expected.

Oh, Dan was quite a character. He left school at 13. "Unlucky for some," he used to say.

He spent most of his early years on the dole. "I got my degree in the University of Life," he explained.

I heard he'd started out as a militant Trotskyist. And a committed pacifist! "Well," he said, "I was a miner's son; I had a bitter hatred of capitalism."

Once I attended a meeting where I heard him speak about his beliefs. As far as I can remember, he said: "Struggle. Revolution. Utopia. Solidarity. Brotherhood of Man.

Dictatorship of the Proletariat. Redistribution of wealth. A rifle is a weapon with a worker at both ends. The workers united shall never be defeated. I have seen the future and it works. Others have tried to understand the world, we are here to change it." The audience were thrilled. And I'd never heard such applause.

By the end of the war, Dan had joined the Labour Party. Mellowed, was how he put it. Gained a bit of wisdom. But, as he always said, he was never the blustering, self-assured individual normally associated with publicity. No, no he was very self-effacing.

When I first met Dan, it was the fresh and vigorous period of the early sixties. Everything I had in sight seemed assured of success. My company was performing miracles throughout the land, turning water into wine, if I may say so. And I was itching to try my skills abroad. We went down to London, Dan and I, and had a little chat in my suite at the Dorchester.

We were drinking Chardonnay. Dan said to me: "Those were the days! I was head of Newcastle Council. I was leader of the local Labour Party. I was chairman of the North East Economic Development Council. Or whatever it was called. Something like that."

Now some people might think Dan Smith was not an obvious partner for someone like me, a leading member of the National Liberal Party, whose wife was President of the Yorkshire Conservative Ladies Section. But, as he himself often said, he was always a good friend to the building trade. He had ambitious plans for the systematic demolition of Newcastle's worst slums which were well advanced. He had fire and enthusiasm. And it was exactly what I myself craved to do with the bombed and rubble-strewn cities of Britain. Replacing the shameful ghettoes of Victorian life with clean, modern blocks and fine open landscapes. Dan had not only the power to make his dream come true, but the ability to make others share his dream. To make *me* share his dream.

One day he said to me: "Brasilia."

That's how he saw Newcastle. The new Brasilia. Oh, he had a messianic flavour. Yes, we were both visionaries. We both believed in a brave new world and would seek any path to reach it! And shortly after we met, by coincidence, I was offered this rather good job at Blyth, just up the coast from Newcastle. I suppose my reputation had preceded me. But then I got a phone call. And I said to Dan: "I understand there's a spot of bother. Some trouble about a housing contract with Newcastle Council. I understand certain papers are being sent to the minister."

He quickly reassured me. "Oh no, it's just a committee motion, John. They're calling for an inquiry, but they won't get it. Two Labour people defected and I lost the vote. Silly buggers. I blame their wives. Jealousy, that's all it is. Nothing will come of it." And nothing did. Except Dan had a heart attack.

But he said to me: "Don't worry, John. It may look bad, but it was only a very *small* heart attack. I get them now and then." Well, I could see he'd made a full recovery. But he said: "I'll tell you this – I am generally a bit run-down these days. I could do with a holiday. You know what I'd really like? A sunshine cruise. That's what my doctor recommended, as a matter of fact. But I have to admit there isn't much cash in the bank right now..."

Well, I could never resist the cry of the sick and the wail of the distressed. So I said to Dan: "You know, when my own batteries run down, it's my habit and policy to take my good lady wife away to the sun for a brief respite. As it happens, I've already arranged a forthcoming trip to Majorca. Why don't you and your own good lady join us? Be my guest. I often find that more can be accomplished sitting in a deck chair than in a busy office."

Afterwards he said to me: "John, I'm a man restored. I don't mind telling you. But I don't want it to happen again, do I? I want to get away from all the politics, all this strain and stress. I've been offered a job. I've been offered this public relations post with a large building firm. It's good money and it'll get me away from the parochial attitude of certain councillors. What do you think?"

I was shocked. "But Dan, you're a leader and an idealist. I think it would be a terrible retrograde step for a man of your talent and ability."

He came back quick as a flash. "In that case, John, why don't *you* employ me?"

When I thought about it, it was an attractive idea. As an architect, I was forbidden to advertise or promote my interests directly. On the other hand, there could be no bar to my using Dan's contacts with housing committees and local councils to gain early knowledge whenever new work was proposed. And Dan could recommend me for interviews and things. "Of course," I said, "there must be no suggestion of favouritism."

And he nodded his head. Quite vigorously. So we knew where we stood.

3. Call me Reggie

WHEN SHE heard all this, Angela said: "Well, that Mr Newcastle seemed a very nice man. And you clearly had a good time in Majorca."

"You may find it hard to believe, but later on, these innocent jaunts would be held against me as evidence of corruption."

She said: "Some people just don't understand about industry and commerce." And I had to agree.

Then she said: "Who's next?"

"Next?"

"Well, that Mr Newcastle is certainly a good character. Colourful. The readers will enjoy him, I'm sure. But we've got to keep up the momentum. You've really known a *lot* of famous people, haven't you?"

Yes. And I had just the man. Let's see if you can guess who it is. He was called to the bar in 1940. When war broke out, he joined RAF Intelligence, for which I believe his first class degree in Greats from Oxford University quite properly fitted him. He was then appointed private secretary to a minister in Mr Churchill's cabinet. In 1960 he became Paymaster General and was influential in setting up the European Free Trade Area. And he very nearly became Prime Minister, being beaten for the Conservative leadership by only 17 votes!

Of course it was Reginald Maudling. The first time I met him, he was guest speaker at a meeting of the National Liberal Party which I had organised. He came onstage in a crumpled suit, carrying a whole sheaf of papers. But then he took one look and said: "I can see we have a very lively audience tonight, an audience who think for themselves, an audience who value spontaneity and straight talking. So! I did make some notes for my speech but I don't think I'll bother with them!" And he tore up all the papers!

And his message was disarmingly forthright. "Free Trade. Enterprise. Money. Prosperity. Profit margins. Workforce. Mobility. Investment. Innovation. Savings. Enterprise. Liquidity. Free Trade. Property-owning democracy. Consumer choice. To govern is to serve. Plan for leisure. Tax relief. Bonus payments. Asset management. Liquidity. Or did I mention liquidity before? Well, if I did, I make no apology for mentioning the subject again."

And afterwards we were sharing a drink and he said: "Call me Reggie if you want, John."

I was impressed by his bigness. Even his handshake was that of a powerful man. And he seemed so relaxed. Afterwards we had a nightcap at the Dorchester. He had an air of complete unconcern, as though affairs of state were no more important than a game of billiards. I said to him: "You know, Reggie, I have some projects developing in several important places – Nigeria, Malta, Angola and the Middle East."

He was obviously impressed. "Gosh, John, you do get around."

I wanted to offer Reggie a job. But I had to be very careful about it. I thought he might consider any offer from *me* as being far beneath him. But I said: "I'm involved with this company called..." I told him the name.

And he said: "I'm happy to be its chairman, John." And we shook hands on it.

And then he said an amazing thing: "One thing I have to tell you, though: I am fearfully lazy. I suppose that's what makes me work so hard. I'd fall asleep if I didn't."

I explained I was involved with a number of companies. I did not actually own any of them but my wife was a shareholder and any architectural work which they obtained was usually passed on to me. "I need someone who is well known and respected overseas. And it's your name that keeps coming back to me from all my contacts." Reggie was held in trust and admiration by everyone of importance. Despite being careless in his dress, he nevertheless communicated an easy-going, donnish authority which flattered many foreigners.

He used to say: "I'm always glad to help the export drive."

As well as Reggie's relaxed charm, the thing which never failed to impress me was his love of alcohol, which he consumed with no apparent effect on speech or performance. I said to him: "This job is a means by which you could do something genuinely constructive for the British position abroad and I will see to it personally that you have a free hand."

For his part, he said: "I do have connections which should be useful for this sort of thing. I'm a director of several merchant banks. But I want you to understand: I won't take a salary."

I was impressed. "Reggie, you're an idealist."

He explained he had a fearful tax problem and simply didn't want to earn any more money. But he was very involved with the theatre. There was a modest little playhouse near where he lived and he was always struggling to raise funds for it. Of course I signed a cheque straight away.

"Make it out to my personal account," said Reggie, "It's easier for me to pass it on to them."

Reggie and I toured Liberia and discussed port projects. He moved easily through the palaces and the pleasure resorts of the Gulf, promising here, reassuring there, always with his own peculiar blend of bonhomie. That spring I also took him to Mexico. At the same time we were invited to design an hotel and casino in Iran. And through Reggie's friendship with certain dignitaries in Dubai, we were invited to prepare three schemes of office blocks as well as an international airport.

So things were looking very bright. But how could I guess what lay ahead? Perhaps I should have been warned by my dealings with so many Arabs. As Reggie said, they simply didn't possess the standards of honesty and straight-dealing known to us here in Britain.

Since then, of course, I have been sadly educated in some diaphanous distinctions. Where a man is, say, a firm believer in the expansion of British trade and influence, it is a tragic epitaph for him to end his career in ignominy and censure through no more than a slight confusion between his personal interests and those of his country.

"Personal interests," said Angela, "And when was it you realised things were going wrong?"

4. A Chat With My Chief Accountant

TOWARDS THE end of 1968, I decided to take stock of my situation. Cash flow was a problem and a quick estimate showed that administrative costs were rising rapidly. In the next year they would face a leap from seven to 28 per cent. Then, on a Monday morning late in June 1969, I was visited in my Pontefract office by my Chief Accountant. He carried a ledger. From his expression, grim enough for a funeral, I expected no more than another disturbing reminder, such as I had received of late, that our costs and expenses would have to be cut back drastically in view of the difficult times we were experiencing.

But he said: "Mr Poulson, I do wish I didn't have to do this. I'm very sorry to have to tell you, but you are insolvent. Unless you find some means of rectifying the position immediately, you will face very serious consequences."

"Surely not?" I said.

"Surely. Yes," he said.

"But no."

"But yes."

"But it cannot be."

"But it is."

I slowly began to realise this was not some strange surrealist dream but an actual happening. I had not previously had the slightest inkling, despite the thicket of problems and disappointments through which we had been struggling. I roused myself. The columns of neat little figures staring up at me looked suddenly sinister. But my first inclination was to laugh at the absurdity.

I said: "These figures don't tell half the story. They can't do. Look, we are owed far more than is shown here, more than we can owe anybody including the Inland Revenue. How can I be insolvent with all that coming in?"

He said: "But it's *not* coming in. You are insolvent to the tune of £100,000 and you will have to find the money immediately if the company is to stay afloat."

I looked at this wretch and laughed again. I wondered how best to enlighten him as to the real situation: one in which I was owed not only £70,000 by Reggie Maudling himself, but half a million more by a major engineering firm. I said: "There have been a few reverses. I am well aware of it. But if things have been allowed to get into this situation, why was I not told before?" I then listed the points for and against. "It is true we have suffered a few unpleasant blows just lately…"

"Quite a few, as it happens. That hospital in Leeds."

I was aware that drawings completed by one of our departments proved faulty and I found it necessary to put another team on the work to pull us out of a hole.

"That set us back £50,000, Mr Poulson. Then there was that hospital in Sussex."

I was aware the work had got mucked about and dithered over by one of those local committees of nincompoops so that in the end we were forced to meet massive setting-up costs – more than our final fees, in fact – before a single brick had been laid…

"And then…" said my Chief Accountant.

I was certainly aware that credit restrictions imposed by a small-minded Labour government had forced a cutback in building work all over the country and held up a number of schools and other projects – a delay which meant we had to pay tax on work for which we had not yet received any fees. No doubt I should have acted ruthlessly much earlier. I still had a large amount to pay the Inland Revenue, but the money which was about to flow in from projects overseas would more than compensate.

"But we have immediate problems," said the Chief Accountant, "And many of those future projects and promised fees you talk about will vanish like smoke once it is known that we are in financial trouble. Mr Maudling…"

"Reggie…" I said.

"Mr Maudling has failed to win the amount of foreign business we anticipated. He has failed to extract fees from the people who employed us to build hospitals in Mexico, where we have so pleasantly and expensively holidayed. I'm sorry, sir. The figures are there. The books don't lie."

I was furious. "Books?" I cried, "What do I know about books? I pay others to keep my books. I pay *you*!"

"And I have kept them, sir. Faithfully."

So I had to accept it. The penny suddenly dropped. I was bankrupt. So much confusing nonsense has been written about me that I must say this. With sincerity. I became a bankrupt because I was falsely led to believe that monies owed to me would be available in time to settle my debts. At no time until the crash would I accept from anybody that I was in any sort of financial trouble.

Such items as account books were not something I bothered myself with, having any number of highly paid staff to deal with them. You must remember that I was often flying round the globe in pursuit of my widespread interests. There was no time to think of such things. If Dan or Reggie or anybody else had a small holiday on my account, why should I bother to measure this against the many millions I was discussing with sheikhs, rulers and presidents around the world? I was carrying out enormous projects both at home and overseas. I was operating a universal enterprise with myriad clients. As I saw it, the factors which finally brought me down were insignificant. Mistakenly, I let others handle them for me.

The scope of my work in the sixties astonishes me even now. I was building a palace for an Arabian Prince on the shores of the Gulf. I was putting up one of the Mediterranean's largest hospitals on the Maltese island of Gozo, for which her gracious majesty Queen Elizabeth the Second laid the foundation stone. I was planning the giant Aviemore Sports and Hotel complex in Scotland. Then there was a school in Nigeria, a harbour in Angola, hundreds of homes, factories and industrial buildings.

When people came to me for trivial affairs like tickets to the Test match at Headingley or an occasional night at the Dorchester, or even an occasional house, I was only too happy to help those less fortunate than I. So I leave it to the world to judge.

But I find that one of the least acceptable aspects of British life is the hunger for scandal feverishly pandered to by the media. Hypocrisy, I believe, is responsible: an odious form which strikes at anyone with wealth as if they were criminals. Every man of means becomes a wicked millionaire by default. Every professional who steps out of line, or is thought to have done so, attracts shocked surprise.

My earnings were perhaps high enough to suggest extreme riches, but my personal life hardly reflected such a thing. I was abundantly tarred with this dirty brush.

"Dirty brush." Angela paused. The click of the typewriter momentarily ceased. "What did you do? When you knew you were bankrupt?"

Only one thought was in my mind: to return to the one warm corner of my life in which I could nurse this terrifying bruise. I went home to my wife and told her. We went over the figures again and again, looking for a way out, desperately seeking any avenue of escape. But there was none. In the next year my wife sold our prize-winning house.

I remained in acute shock. You see, the thing was that all my companies and assets were actively trading, still contracted to carry out enormous projects. All that was needed to save me was for a few of these to come to fruition. All that was needed was a bridge of money to bring me safely to dry land. Perhaps there were friends who could help me out, albeit temporarily. But, to my grave disappointment, no such offer was forthcoming.

If I had never accepted bankruptcy, the evidence of any so-called corruption would never have come out. I would never have caused such a stir in government circles that I had to be arrested and made a political prisoner! Never would I have had to face the terrible threat of assassination. Yes, murder! That is the threat I now face.

"Ooh," said Angela, "now that's something for the readers. No sex then. But maybe a bit of violence. That's something to look forward to."

I assumed it was another of her jokes.

5. Bankrupt

ON THE morning when I filed my petition for bankruptcy, there was not a penny to my name. My solicitor drove me to the Official Receiver in Leeds, adjoining the offices of the Board of Trade. I remember little of that visit. Life now seemed full of unpleasant visits. And I can remember very few of them.

And prior to that, I had tried to run away. I had resolved to disappear to Ireland from where I could, perhaps, recoup some honour and fortune to my battered estate.

It was a dark December morning. I took the Mini – the one remaining means of transport available to me – and drove towards London. My mind was seething, a great wave of sorrow blinded me to the folly of my plan. In an act of complete abandon, the duties and principles of my upbringing, of my family and church, were to be flung away as if they did not exist. But fate deals strange cards in the game of life. In the event, after I had already bought my ticket for passage across the sea to Fishguard, I chose to phone a friend, who said to me: "It's not like you, John, to cut and run." And he was right. And so I went home.

Even now, I regret the bankruptcy. I believe I could have found ways to avoid it. The figures were both wrongly assessed and ill kept in some scrappy books maintained by some of my staff. Had there been an adequate accounting system and a greater emphasis placed on the collection of debts, then I truly believe we could have emerged from the financial ditch without a broken bone. I was owed more than £1 million when I was first approached by the Inland Revenue for those enormous unpaid income taxes and National Insurance contributions.

The knowledge that I still had a number of outstanding fees covering my work on the Saudi hospital, two others in Mexico, and one in Iran had prevented any worry.

Then, on the night of Friday 22 June 1973, I heard a ring at the door of our now modest little bungalow and found a plain clothes police officer.

After identifying himself, he said: "John Garlick Poulson, I have a warrant for your arrest. And I must warn you that anything you say may be taken down and used in evidence against you." I was numb with shock.

The Detective said: "You are probably numb with shock, sir. Most people are. Come with me."

They took me to a foul little hole, the floor covered with urine and dusted over with disinfectant, with only a dirty grey blanket and a plank for bedding.

The Detective said: "I know it doesn't look like much. But let me tell you we are giving you the rare privilege of using a cell normally reserved for women." The men's cells apparently were filled with the usual Friday night drunks who tended to be rather noisy and abusive. Next morning I was relieved to be granted bail.

I was being charged with conspiring to corrupt government officials. My friend George Pottinger, having suffered a similar arrest, was also brought along. He was wearing shorts.

He said: "They came to my bloody tennis club. The nerve of these fellas!"

It was so cheering to see him. "Oh George, do you remember that night when our dream of building the Aviemore ski resort had foundered so dramatically? Do you remember when we discovered that J Arthur Rank had bought the land? Oh what a sad bunch we were, what a dismal party as we boarded the train for London. Mulling over our failure."

"Drinking Bell's whisky."

"I may have had the odd glass."

"All the way to London."

"But we picked ourselves up, George. I met you two days later and we said we'd go ahead anyway on a different site. I built a new model. A hotel with 100 rooms. A perfect complex of shopping, hotel and sporting facilities, all set in scenic splendour. I never got a penny for my work."

"I remember that model. You could look in all the windows. Was it real glass?"

"No, no. Cellophane."

"It looked real. Looking in windows. Just like real life. It was an excellent model."

But our chit-chat was interrupted when the clerk of court asked for our pleas. Of course, we both pleaded: Not Guilty.

George said: "Don't worry, John. There is absolutely no case to answer." Then he said: "Right. I'm off to finish my game. I intend to enjoy my bail, John, and so should you. You worry too much." George so loved his tennis. And his manner was so cheering.

But, as the day for my criminal trial came closer, I began to lose my hopeful spirits. I knew I was innocent of everything except stupidity. But I knew the weight of every shred of evidence, my most unselfish and sincerest acts of Christian charity, would be used against me. There were people out to get me. The world I believed in and sought to cherish with acts of kindness turned its stony face on me.

And I want to tell you about the time I tried to kill myself. The police, the law, and much of the world had come to see me as a man who obtained work by bribery and corruption. But if this were so, why was I now gasping for commissions to offset the continuing drain on my finances, the incessant demands from my creditors? At home I had the unpleasant task of paying off my domestic staff. Where before I had entertained freely – though never lavishly, as was dishonestly reported by many newspapers – the sackcloth of austerity now prevailed. The horrible pressures of adversity in everything I touched had finally destroyed my nerve. Only those who have had their innermost feelings stretched on the rack could understand these corroding doubts which tormented my days and nights.

For years I had been using a sleeping drug, sodium amytal, to help me rest during long air journeys. I took it now as a refuge from my dark thoughts. I had been warned by my doctor never to exceed three tablets. That I possessed such an easy escape route from all my troubles became a nagging temptation in the back of my mind. Finally, I decided to end my life.

My wife and I were staying in our London flat. She was spending the day at the Conservative Women's conference, so I was alone from soon after breakfast. I was depressed and in a low state of health. Some premonition on the part of my wife prompted her to return immediately after the meeting, though the stores of Piccadilly surely beckoned. I was lying in a coma after swallowing 22 tablets. My life hung on a very slender thread. But, with God's grace, I pulled through.

And still the demands from creditors came in. Though I was technically impoverished and living off my wife, and unable even to afford pipe tobacco without the sustenance of my brother, still people were claiming I owed them a percentage of this, a fraction of that...

In the weeks and months of my ordeal, the media hounds camped on the road in front of our bungalow and used every ruse to grub up a story. These stories were invariably false and distorted. I discovered that a Deputy Commander at New Scotland Yard – codenamed Charlie Fox – had been interviewing Reggie Maudling in an operation colourfully known as Charlie Fox Fiddle. Dan Smith was quickly brought to trial in the sort of publicity he had never been able to achieve on *my* behalf – despite all the money I paid him. And – amazingly – he pleaded *guilty*! I was stunned. What on earth could have made him do that?

I was now the nation's Aunt Sally. I was learning that the system of British justice I had so admired was not always a fine idealistic absolute, but that lawyers make deals and trade off one situation against another. I had previously believed only electricians and second-hand car salesmen were capable of such behaviour. Even now, the ordeal I endured at my trial and the equally horrendous torment of my bankruptcy hearing fill me with the horror of a nightmare.

Judges, magistrates, barristers. They would ask me about the way my company's books were kept. And I had admit the highly paid staff I employed had created a shambles. Items were wrongly entered. The reasons for them were not always correct. I found various sums of money were missing entirely.

I was asked about companies people believed I owned and I had to say I was not directly connected with any one of them. Though it is true that my wife held shares in some of the other companies, my only interest, and I can say this with sincerity, was in being retained by them for the occasional job. There was nothing improper in this, rather the reverse. It was a legal and ethical way in which I could increase my scope and expansion.

But now these judges, magistrates and barristers would press me for details – more, I think, to make a name for themselves than to elicit any significant truth.

They showed me a long schedule of monies paid to people on my behalf. One of the barristers said: "It is plain, is it not, Mr Poulson, that you are a man with an immensely generous heart?"

For a brief moment I truly believed that someone had finally understood. But then I realised it was sarcasm.

They pointed out that, while insolvent, I had paid Dan Smith £22,000 as a consultant in housing. They pointed out that I had paid George Pottinger £19,000 in the same period. They seemed to imply there was some connection between these payments to George and the fact that he was a high-ranking official. I replied, as any free-born Englishman would, that surely I could give whatever I liked to whomever I liked.

At one point, my legs became suddenly weak and dizziness clouded my brain. I fainted. In any case, my general health had deteriorated. For some time I had been bothered by recurrent, violent debilitating colitis. My diseased arm had been paining me more than normal. Gout was bedevilling my movements. Was there now, as well as these nagging ailments, a more sinister organism attacking my health and strength – perhaps even a fatal sickness of mind or heart?

When I spoke to my solicitor, he advised me that I should avoid argument with learned counsel. I must state the facts as simply as possible and no more. This he drilled into me: *on no account must I allow myself to become engaged in an emotional wrangle*. Well, I certainly did my best.

One of the barristers even asked me if I was at odds with my wife. That really raised my hackles, I can tell you. But I stayed calm. He said: "Mr Poulson, are you trying to make out that you are a sort of timid, easily shockable man? There you are, living in the same house, and never asking her what she has done with several thousands of pounds worth of assets. It doesn't sound very sensible."

But if I were feeling low, what about Reggie Maudling? The Prime Minister had already announced in the House of Commons that, as a result of disclosures made in the public examination, together with a report from the Official Receiver, the City of London Metropolitan Fraud Squad had been instructed to carry out an investigation. He had therefore reluctantly and regretfully accepted the resignation of his Home Secretary.

I did not realise just then that Maudling's departure had shaken the very foundations of the establishment. Any reflection of Reggie's scandal on other members of the cabinet would spell disaster. No party in power could survive it. I now know that the tremors of panic running through the cabinet office were to have the most disastrous results for me. What I am about to reveal will no doubt sound far-fetched, if not fantastic, perhaps even the vengeful imaginings of a bitter mind. But it is the only logical explanation for my imprisonment.

The evidence was brought to me voluntarily by a man whose identity I cannot reveal, even today. What this retired official has told me proves beyond doubt that I was the victim of a wave of panic sweeping through the highest echelons of the Conservative government. There was enough dynamite, so they believed, to destroy their power. So the word went out: *Poulson must be the one who pays the price!*

6. The Price

"JOHN GARLICK Poulson, the magnitude and evil nature of what you have done is such that I have not taken into account your age or your health or the fact that in your case, this has been hanging over you for more than two years…"

That was what the Judge said. When they found me guilty.

So I ended up with seven years! My wife wanted to appeal, outraged that age and health should have been dismissed so abruptly. In fact, we *did* appeal. But it was dismissed despite many cogent grounds. The Judge's pronouncement confirmed my conviction that understanding is not part of the process of the law. What it wants is a victim, somebody to get its teeth into. A scapegoat. But plenty of others beside myself have found it hard to accept that verdict or the foolish notion of me as an evil man. *The Guardian* said next morning that I was a peculiarly

Dickensian figure: at my best a Mr Pickwick; when my debts piled up, a Mr Micawber; and the writers added that, like Mr Pecksniff, I never suspected that my world would come crashing down. Well, it was the first time ever that I had been compared to the great figures of English literature and it is a pity that I have had to suffer so much for such an accolade! At least they could never compare me to Scrooge!

Angela said: "What's the difference between a jeweller and a jailor?"

In truth, I had no idea.

"One sells watches, the other watches cells." She sighed. "Go on. Tell us about prison."

One expects a place of punishment to be grim. To me the tragic revelation of imprisonment is the utter spiritual emptiness of it. There are few inmates whom I would describe as totally useless. Yet, to my profound depression, there is in all but the tiniest minority an absolute indifference to any form of spiritual life, faith or even hope, such as normal people like you and I experience.

Never in my life has my own religious discipline proved so valuable. I thank God daily for my faith. In the event, I have done three years of my sentence and am now ready to be released. And I can say without fear of contradiction: prison is useless. It does not reform. It does not rehabilitate. Still less does it offer any acceptable belief that those forced to suffer captivity will emerge without further taint of spiritual coarseness from the bad habits of the inmates. In my opinion far too much of our prison system is confined to the control of prisoners, not nearly enough to their salvation. Fear is the most vicious contributor to this helplessness.

I suppose I have to admit there *are* some proper and legitimate ways to pass the time. I myself joined a language class to learn Italian. I had always enjoyed Latin at school and had pleasant memories of my visits to the Mediterranean and the Adriatic. But most prisoners have no time for linguistics.

At Christmas there is much making of hooch – bootleg liquor to assuage and compensate for the pangs of spending Christmas inside. Every imaginable method of producing alcohol is tried, every conceivable place of hiding is used. One prisoner used the hollow legs of his steel chair as a still to store the fermenting fruit juices. But the resulting gas blew off the rubber stoppers, so he lost it all. And, I have to say, he also deposited a flood of evil-smelling liquid over the floor.

Fires started by prisoners are a constant hazard. To my own distress, one of the most popular targets is the chapel. Oh yes. And I have to tell you the class system within society is also reflected within the prison. Deep divisions exist between those who share criminal backgrounds and are mostly illiterate, and those who are political prisoners, such as I am. A man of education and refinement is automatically a target of abuse and ribaldry from the moment he enters the prison gates.

I was, of course, something of a star attraction for visitors. So I had to endure the indignity of the peep show. When visitors were conducted round the workshops and communal rooms, I was pointed out as an object of particular interest: John Poulson, the corrupt architect.

Oh, I was to have a prison visitor of my own at one time. But word reached me – I cannot name the source – that the two men from whom I was to choose were both under instruction to report back everything I told them. Once I knew this, I of course declined.

Recently the news has come through – I am to be paroled after three and a quarter years! I am not bitter. I say that with all sincerity. The price I paid was demanded of me by a society in which, too often, a scapegoat has to be provided.

But I believe the prison system I have endured is the quintessence of evil. The calculated cruelty of locking away virile men in total segregation from the opposite sex is more than a punishment. It creates a society of animal needs, reducing men to levels of immorality and lust which have no counterpart in the outside world. Blackmail and the traffic in homosexual favours flourish. As our great Lord Hailsham has written, British prisons are a university of crime!

On many occasions I was witness to violence and trouble-making. But I was at least reassured by the fact that there were teams of crack sharp-shooters standing by to deal with incidents.

"Violence!" said Angela, "At last."

"Violence?" I said, "*You* know nothing of violence, Miss Record. Now I will tell you about the attempt to murder me." She was silent then and I could see I had shocked her.

How the attempt was to be executed was revealed to me by a trusted prison officer who also shall remain nameless. I was on my way back to work that morning when I saw him beckoning me from a doorway.

"Poulson," he said, "your life is in danger. Apart from me, only the chief medical officer and the governor know about this."

I was understandably startled. "The governor? Do you mean the governor of this prison?"

"Well, I don't mean the bloody Bank of England," he said, though the word he used was not *bloody*. "Listen. You must on no account drink anything not prepared by yourself."

"Are you saying someone is trying to poison me?"

"Not poison. Drugs. I have been sitting up for the past three nights with an inmate under sedation. He has babbled it all out to me. Somehow he has managed to smuggle eight LSD tablets in with him. And they are intended for you. He wants to make you take your own life."

"But I would never do such a thing. How could he think…?"

He turned away briefly and it seemed to me for a moment that he was laughing at me. But I now believe he was worried about being overheard. "At the moment, the plan is to dope your cup of tea. It is known that you like your tea, Poulson, and you like it milky."

"I do indeed," I said, "I have a special ration of two pints of milk a day for health reasons."

"The idea is that it will make you believe you can fly – and you will then jump off a top landing."

I knew this man was never one to exaggerate. "But why should anyone wish to kill me?"

"It's what they've been saying in the papers. They're saying that when you get out, you will tell all."

"Tell all? All of what?"

"That you will name names, big men, top men, men above suspicion, men whose innocence has never been questioned." He started to walk off. "You look after yourself, Poulson."

All that day my hand shook as I tried to concentrate on my work. It so happened at that time I was involved in some quite interesting work helping to manufacture board games. Monopoly, Cluedo, that sort of thing. It used to be a joke among us that we could steal some get-out-of-jail-free cards.

Three or four days later I was told that the would-be assassin had been transferred to another prison. I never discovered how he had managed to bring the LSD tablets into the prison. But if *he* could do it, why not others? I still wake with a shiver when I remember that everything I touch, or put to my lips, may contain a lurking threat. Lest anyone think this story is a product of my imagination, let me tell you that a lawyer whom I shall not name was able to confirm that he had been told such a story by a social worker whom he was unwilling to identify.

Also at this time I was offered a temptation and I was sorely tempted indeed. I had spent some time in the prison hospital. A good-looking young man who was put into a bed near mine, and with whom I passed some hours in conversation, claimed to have worked in the French underworld with the infamous Jackal. I was inclined to believe him. He spoke with a Liverpool accent.

And to prove it, he showed me his legs, scarred with knife wounds. They were strong handsome legs apart from the scars. Then he asked if I wanted anyone *looked after*. Yes, that was the phrase he used. I listened with horror as he explained he meant *murdered*. If I would make out a list, he told me solicitously, he would dispatch every name on it for £200 apiece upon his release. I was indeed tempted, bearing in mind the danger I was in; but in the end, I could not go ahead with it.

I have since written down the name of this man. I will only say in my book that I have deposited it where it is easily accessible to men of the law. But I will not reveal it now.

7. George

I WAS never one of those who bemoans his lot. What has kept me going through these troubled times is that I was happy once and my discipline is to remember those happy times. With my daughters. With my wife. With my friend George.

What can I say about George? What can I say of this man I so admired? No human being is perfect. I believe he felt himself well above petty necessities and restrictions. He felt such things were for lesser mortals.

One day we were having a very pleasant time driving in his car and he said: "My old Volvo is well past it, John. Don't you think?"

"Oh, it's got a few years yet."

"I was thinking I could do with a new Rover."

"Well, as it happens, it is my occasional practice to provide motorcars to my senior staff. I'll see you get one."

He said: "You're too generous." He had clearly never intended to ask for money and was made almost speechless by my offer.

"No, no. It's only because my accountants are hammering away at me to spend more to reduce taxation. I would be delighted if you would accept."

"In that case, you've twisted my arm, John. And that's a dangerous thing to do when a man's driving. Therefore I accept."

I actually never intended it as a gift, only a long-term loan. But the bankruptcy court clearly had no experience of a loan without strings, interest, signature or seal. My laws of generosity are my own.

And another time I was visiting him at home. We had just enjoyed a glass of Sauvignon and George was showing me round. "Well, here it is, John. My lovely house. You've been damned generous about this house, John. I never imagined you would take on so much. First you bought the land..."

"It's only a small piece of land," I said, "Only big enough to build a small house."

"Well, small-*ish*! And I'm so grateful." Then he hugged me. I was quite embarrassed.

"Well, it was a long time since I'd built a house. There are so many bigger things in my life right now..."

"And the mortgage..."

"What's the point of being director of a building society if you can't help people with their mortgage?"

136

"And of course I will repay you. All of it. Eventually."

"It's nothing. A gesture of goodwill towards a man who is a very special and admired friend. There's certainly no hurry."

"Thank you, John. Thank you so much." We were in the hallway and he pointed at the floor. "Isn't that an extraordinary mosaic, John? Isn't it marvellous? Those three pelicans beneath your feet are the official insignia of the Orkneys, where I was born. I've always wanted to celebrate the place. And I thought a lovely mosaic in the entrance hall would do just that. And celebrate our friendship too."

I could not begrudge him. If three pelicans made him happy, the money spent seemed little enough.

After my bankruptcy hearing and after I tried to kill myself, I went to stay with George for a brief but pleasant time in the home I had built for him. He was, as always, urbane, detached and consoling. He said there was no threat to my ultimate livelihood; certainly none that I could not overcome in time.

A little later I received through the post a small outstanding bill headed *Mosaic: Orkney*.

Had either of us guessed the grave construction later to be put on this bill by the prosecution, we would not have been so careless and stupid.

Then one day he said: "John, I'm going to change my defence."

"I don't understand. Change your defence? What on earth do you mean?"

"Oh, don't worry. It's only a legal manoeuvre. You see, it is true that the civil service has certain – how shall I put it? – esoteric rules of conduct. And I do now realise, I do now acknowledge, that I have broken some of those rules. I've been greedy, John."

"No, George. Not you. You could never take bribes any more than I could *give* bribes. If I had a son, I would want him to be like you. I have always wanted to help you, to give you what is so easy for me: a few favours, loans, holidays and so forth. What I do for you is little enough."

"But I *have* been greedy, John. I've been bad. Rules of conduct, John. Rules."

I look back and remember them all.

Dan Smith was a weak, weak man. The last time I saw him before he went to prison, he went down on his bended knees and begged me to believe that he had told the investigators nothing but good of me. But he was lying, as usual.

And Reggie Maudling! I went on paying for that damned theatre trust of his a long time after it folded. Curtain down, you might say, on a long-running pantomime. But, of course, the cheques were always made out to Reggie and of course he kept cashing them!

But George Pottinger is still a man I am happy to know. Disgrace has not embittered him. Even in prison, he remains the top-drawer Scot, an upper-crust Edinburgh aristocrat to his fingertips. Whatever the plea, whatever history may choose to say about him, George Pottinger was entirely innocent of anything but foolishness. He never conspired about anything. I excuse him. I feel he is more sinned against than sinning, a man whose one fault – his boyish vanity – may well have betrayed him. To me, George Pottinger was, and is, the most exceptional man I have ever met.

8. Posterity

ANGELA SAID: "Well, you're a strange person, Mr P. I don't know how to take you sometimes."

"A strange person? Well, I *am* a convicted felon, Miss Record, an undischarged bankrupt sent to prison for conspiring to corrupt, in many minds a monstrous crook who twisted the arms of illustrious people to his own grasping advantage. But I think it is clear to anyone who will read my book that I have no need to justify anything. Should you not be typing this?"

"Oh yes," she said and started typing furiously.

"I have been a blind fool. I lost control of my sense of Christian charity, my natural generosity in giving presents, holidays, gifts of money and motorcars to those with whom I associated. It had not seemed wrong to me at the time – to be so lavish, to provide such gifts to civil servants who were prevented by archaic rules from publicly accepting them. Ah, this was indeed the worst kind of folly. But dishonest? No. Corrupting?

No. Evil? No. My mistake was to do too much too fast. I had a vision of Britain sliding the wrong way in a world of aggressive progress, and I wanted to set it right. With my large and sophisticated organisation, I believed I could offset the terrible malaise which was destroying our once glittering nation."

"Glittering nation," she said.

"I will tell you what I mean about the British malaise. You remember I told you that Queen Elizabeth the Second and Prince Philip, the Duke of Edinburgh, came to Malta to honour my work by laying the foundation stone for my hospital. Well, there was a hollow and revealing blank on the ceremonial stone where the name of the building contractor should have been. Later, when Prince Philip asked me the name of the contractor, I had to admit that no-one had yet been appointed. I explained that Reggie Maudling should have informed the Palace. But clearly he had not done so. The Monarch of Great Britain had declared the hospital building in progress when nobody had been retained to add a single extra brick to that wall."

"Oh, walls. Well, life's full of walls, isn't it? Just look at this place." Then she said: "You look tired, Mr P. I think we'd better finish for the day, don't you?"

I protested. "But I enjoy it. I enjoy the work. I do. And I enjoy your company." Without thinking about it, I took her hand.

"I know I'm a great comfort," she said, "It's my sense of humour."

"And the book is very important. I'm going to call it *The Price* because of the price I have paid to write it. It will set the record straight. Before I die."

"Mr P, I can see into the future. Did you know that?"

"Oh really?" I managed to laugh. "And what do you predict?"

"I predict your friend George, who loves his tennis, will die on a tennis court."

I almost laughed again.

Then fear gripped me. "The future isn't something I have much of, is it?" I said. And then: "Oh Spirit! It is you I fear the most. You are about to show me shadows of the things to come, the things that have not yet happened but will do so! Is that not so?"

She picked up the teapot that seemed to have appeared along with the kettle. "Nothing so dramatic, Mr P. It's not humbug! It's all in the tealeaves. Now I'll tell you what I see." She paused. "Oh! Your book will never be published."

I said: "I don't understand."

"There will be problems. Legal problems. Briefs will be briefed. Barristers will form a barrier. It's not just *people* who get arrested, you know. Sometimes books get arrested too."

Despair engulfed me. "All for nothing! Oh God, I'm tired. You're right. I'm so tired."

She said: "Then rest. Why not? Everybody rests in the end. Don't be afraid of it."

I lay back and closed my eyes.

Then I opened them again with a start. "My arm! My arm! It doesn't hurt any more."

"Well, that's a Godsend. Now do as you're told. Go to sleep."

"Yes," I said, "I might. I just might. Yes. I feel I could."

This time I couldn't keep my eyes open. And it seemed to me I was no longer on a bunk bed in a prison cell but in my own bed in my modest bungalow which had never won any prizes.

But I still heard her pull the sheet out of the typewriter.

"All that work!" she said, "Can't let it go to waste, can we? Will no-one hear you, Mr P? Will no-one know? One day, I'm sure they will. You get to sleep now, Mr P. I'll be on my way. Well, the job's done, isn't it?"

Then, said Christian, what means this? The angel explained: A little distance from this gate there is erected a strong castle, of which Satan is the captain. From thence, he and his acolytes shoot arrows at those who come up to this gate, so they may die before they can enter into eternal bliss. Then, said Christian, I do both tremble and rejoice. I do tremble for fear of death and rejoice that the host of the Lord will protect and succour me.

Till My Eyes Bleed

THE VOICE on the Tannoy said: "The 13.05 to Leeds will depart from platform four, calling at Peterborough, Grantham, Newark Northgate, Doncaster, Wakefield Westgate and Leeds. Platform four for the 13.05 to Leeds."

Mel was walking across to the platform when he bumped shoulders with a tall, elegantly dressed middle-aged man. They spoke simultaneously.

"Gosh. I'm sorry," said Mel.

"Can't you fuckin look?" said the other.

And then recognition.

"Adie! It's Adie!" And it was! Adrian Merchant. They'd been to the same school.

"Young Mel Simmons! As I live and breathe! My God, you young streak of vomit, it's been years!"

And it was true. Years and years and years. They'd not seen each other for... well, years and years. Mel felt so guilty! All he could say was: "Well!"

Adie said: "Well, well, this calls for a celebration. Fortunately, the station hostelry is here at hand!"

"Agh!"

"Agh?"

"What?"

"You said Agh!"

"Yes. Agh! I mean, I'd very much like to but my train is about to leave," Mel looked at his watch, "in three minutes."

"Oh that's a shame. Which train is it?

"Leeds."

"Still in... ?"

"Leeds."

"The provinces."

"Yes. You...?"

"Oh I live here, voodoo child. In London. The smoke. The Big Avocado as I like to call it. Hub of the known universe. Still, Leeds was always very nice."

"Yes."

"A quickie perhaps? Surely? One for the rail?"

"Well..."

"Those trains to Leeds are extremely frequent. So I'm given to understand. Probably more frequent than is strictly necessary."

And that was it. He couldn't just bugger off home, could he? Not with the trains being so frequent. "OK. What'll you have?"

THEY WERE running side by side across the open field. The rest of the boys were up ahead, out of sight. That was no novelty for Mel. But running alongside Adrian Merchant definitely *was*.

Merchant said: "There can't be anything in life more boring than cross-country running." His easy, well-modulated voice belied the exertion of the race.

Mel said: "Oh, do you think so? I think it's quite good really. Better than running round the gym."

Merchant rolled his eyes. "Better than running round the gym. Yes, you certainly have a point there, young'un." Merchant was a year older than Mel. "I suppose you're very much into nature, aren't you, young... What is it you call yourself?"

Mel told him. He already knew who Merchant was. Of course. Editor of the lower school newspaper. Captain of the under-13s rugby team. Winner of the Wesley St John prize for the best annual essay on sportsmanhip. Even at 12, even in running shorts, there was a striking elegance about tall, blond Merchant.

"I suppose, young Simmons, you being the outdoor type, you'll be one of those lads who like birds and flowers and trees, won't you? Want to be a mountain climber when you leave school, eh?"

"Oh no, Merchant. I want to go into business. Like my dad."

"What's he do exactly?"

"Well, not a lot right now." After a pause: "Actually, he's dead."

"Oh. Poor boy. Orphan of the storm."

"It's only because of the insurance that I was able to come to St Wystan's."

"Well then, saved from a bog-standard comprehensive. God *does* exist after all."

After a while Mel said: "What does *your* dad do?"

"At the moment he's doing three years for fraudulent conversion. So I'm a bit of an orphan too."

"Oh. I'm sorry. And what do *you* want to do? When *you* leave school?"

"Write the great novel. Or be the Poet Laureate. Or paint. Politics maybe. And always be rich and beautiful. But look. Enough of this profound philosophical stuff, young reprobate. You can do me a bit of a favour..."

Merchant stopped running. Mel stopped running. Merchant took a packet of Marlboroughs out of the top of his shorts. He said: "Look, if I go behind that tree, I can have a quick drag and you can keep watch." He pulled a cigarette out of the packet. "You just make sure Old Spooner doesn't catch me at it."

Old Spooner was the head of sixth. He liked to run behind the boys and keep watch. Mel said: "So what'll you give me if I do?" He was no mug. He had no intention of getting into trouble with Old Spooner. Not unless he got something out of it. And there was no point Merchant offering him a cigarette because he didn't smoke. "I don't smoke, you know." He thought it was stupid to take risks with your health. He counted himself lucky he wasn't a smoker by nature.

Merchant thought for a moment. "I will give you my friendship for life. And if I should ever betray you, let you down in any way, which God forbid..."

"Yes?"

"Then I shall kill myself."

AND THAT, as Mel often related in times to come, was that! Friends for life. That was something you had to take seriously. So every time they did cross-country running, Mel would look out for Old Spooner and Merchant would have his ciggy. The trouble was they'd waste a lot of time and Mel would always end up last. But Merchant was a natural. He could go from nought to 60 in two seconds flat. The smoking didn't seem to damage his health at all. So he always made the cross-country team anyway and Mel never did. Which Mel thought was unfair. The cross-country team got to go on runs all over Yorkshire and sometimes people came to watch. Girls, actually. *Girls* came to watch. But Merchant said: "You wouldn't like it, young Simmons. It's boring. All those birds and flowers and trees. You wouldn't like it at all. We know you're not a mountain-climber."

They did not go to the same college. They did not even go to different colleges in the same city. Mel stayed in Leeds. But they were still mates, hung around together during vacations. Chilled out, as people say nowadays.

ADIE CAME out in his underpants, a graceful slim figure for all the long, untidy hair and two days' growth of beard. He said: "Mel, Mel, Mel! Is it the middle of the night? Is it really? Have I slept the clock round? You shouldn't have let me."

Mel said: "No, no. It's morning. I just haven't opened the curtains yet. Honest. Here! Look!" And he pulled open the frayed velvet curtains of his student flat. "I wouldn't let you miss out on the sunshine, Adie."

Adie fell back, rubbing his eyes frantically. "Have a heart, young Mel! Have a heart, you cock-sucking dwarf!" Yes, Adie always did have a way with words. But he was only being friendly. "Can't you see I'm a tiny bit under the weather? What sort of rotgut have you been feeding me?"

"Just the regular stuff, Adie. OK, it's not the dearest in the supermarket. But it's not that Netto crap either." Mel was only a student after all, living on his government loan. And he considered his life as very bohemian. Just because he was reading company law didn't mean he'd sold out to the military industrial complex. Adie probably thought *he* had more street cred just because he went to art school and wore long overcoats. "Here, it is a bit on the bright side, isn't it?" Mel pulled the curtains shut again.

"Not the Netto, eh? Not the Netto in the ghetto. Well, that's something for which to be vaguely thankful. I suppose Sainsbury's Glen Campbell or Asda's Infamous Grouse is at least one step in the right direction!" Adie went across to where his jeans hung on the edge of a sofa and rummaged through the pockets. " God, I've run out of cigarettes. You don't...? No, of course not. I'd momentarily forgotten." He slouched over to the table, picked up a dirty glass and eyed it suspiciously. "Is this your breakfast, young Mel?

"Oh no. I'm strictly a black coffee man in the mornings, Ade. Coffee and cornflakes."

"Black coffee sounds excellent. You don't have a drop of that Asda stuff left, do you? Just to take the sting out of the caffeine."

"I might have a drop under the stairs. I'll go and look."

"You mean next to the gas meter?"

"Yeah, that's right."

"Ah. No, I'm afraid you don't. *Not any more.* Don't you remember, young person? I stumbled on a bottle or two at the end of the night. Quite a surprise to find it there, but I suppose if you don't have a cellar…"

"It's because I've joined a Christmas club, you see. So I get some of my drink in early and store it…"

"Christmas clubs are rather working class, aren't they? But you don't have to apologise. Surely we've been friends long enough?"

AND THEN the years rolled by. And they moved apart. And Mel was 40, which made Adie 41 or 42. And now they went into the bar at Kings Cross Station. They got themselves a small table and Mel got two large whiskies.

Adie said: "I'm awfully sorry about the train thing. I really am. Usually they're very frequent. Take my word. But now I think about it, I believe there has been some work on the line. A wood pigeon flew into an overhead cable. Something like that. That probably accounts for it." He lit a cigarette.

"That's Ok. Really. Two and a half hours isn't that long."

"Attaboy!" Adie punched his arm. "Well, my young artichoke, you certainly look every inch the successful… what is it? Businessman?"

"Sort of. I'm a legal adviser in intellectual property."

"You mean flats for students?"

"No. No. You see it's all about copyright and merchandising rights and…" Suddenly he twigged. "Oh. Right.

Yes. That's quite funny. But it *is* very interesting. Well, it *can* be."

"I'm sure it can. And rewarding in other ways..."

"It's not just the money."

"Oh no."

"Though there's plenty of that, Ade. Intellectual property just grows and grows. It's practically the only thing that *does* grow in our cyberspace culture. Apart from *actual* property, of course. What my American friends call *real estate*. That'll always go up, whatever the economic situation."

"Of course."

"Since the EC laws extending the period of copyright and asserting the moral right of the artist and/or licensee..." Mel caught himself. "But no, it's *not* just the money. I mean, when you're dealing with people like Chris Martin and Amy Winehouse..."

"You deal with Chris and Amy? That's fascinating. They've never mentioned you."

"Ah, no. I mainly deal with Safeways and Kwikfit. But I liked that joke about flats for students. Yes, I'll have to tell Beatrice that one."

"Beatrice?"

"My wife actually."

"My God! You're married! Young Melvin is married. I can't believe it! How on earth did that happen? Are you both in intellectual property? That would be quite a coincidence."

"Not quite. She's in human resources. But it's on the legal side."

"Not *illegal* human resources then? Not body parts on the black market?"

This time Mel saw the joke and allowed himself a grin.

"You two must have a lot to talk about," said Adie.

So Mel told him all about it, about Beatrice and him.

MEL WAS taking a break from his course on Management, Law and the Post-Industrial Economy. He got himself a coffee in the cafeteria and saw her sitting at a table reading *Marie Claire*. She was in her thirties, with a good – if rather full – figure, large dark eyes and coal-black hair, a page-boy cut with a fringe.

"I couldn't help noticing..." he began.

"Noticing?" She looked up from an article on *What British Women Think of Their Bodies.* Mel could see instantly it was lavishly illustrated with photographs of naked women.

"Noticing you."

"I didn't see *you.*"

"I was at the back. I always prefer to sit at the back. You get the chance to look around, you get a good view."

"You got a good view of *me,* did you?"

Mel hesitated. "Well, I don't mean I was particularly looking at *you...*"

"You were just looking at the women in general?" She seemed amused. At least she didn't turn back to the pictures.

"Oh no, I'm not the sort of man who looks at women. Well, I *do* look at women. I mean, I'm not gay or anything. No, I *do* look at women. Quite a bit of the time. No, what I mean is..."

"...you weren't particularly interested in *me.*"

"Yes. No. I mean I did find you..."

"Attractive?"

This was the moment. But he was too embarrassed to take it. "Interesting."

"*Not* attractive then."

"Er.. yes. Yes. Attractive. I was just sort of groping for the word."

"I suppose groping for words is about all the groping you ever get to do."

He knew it was an insult but also that it wasn't *really.* So that was it. They had clicked. She was the one who invited *him* out. They went to The Nip in the Bud, the Japanese vegetarian restaurant in Boar Lane. And afterwards – and remember it was the very first time they went out – they went back to her *en suite* room at the Cosy Cottage Hotel. By the morning, he felt, they were pretty much a couple. She told him she'd had this lengthy relationship with a married man but it came to an end when his wife got pregnant again.

She said: "I just made up my mind about you. In the first half hour. I'm the wrong side of 35 and a girl's got to take her chances as they come."

Love at first sight, thought Mel.

ADIE WAS calling out to him. "If they've run out of Tomatin, it'll have to be Johnnie Walker. Beggars can't be choosers, young arsehole."

Mel's marital announcement had in turn precipitated some detailed revelations about Adie's sex life. When Mel came back to the table, Adie said: "This last girl…"

"Samantha?"

"No. Alicia."

"The blonde with the big…"

"No, that was Kathy."

"Right."

"Alicia is the one works in PR. The trouble was…"

"Was..?"

Adie was slurring his words now. "…she was too good for me. Just too bloody good for me. They're all too good for me. I can't live up to their standards."

"Right."

"Can't do it."

"Right."

"Women."

"Right."

"I try. I really do. But some skirt comes into the office… Advertising is like that, you know. You get the top drawer totty. Models."

"Models. Right. And you're the artist…"

"Designer. I'm a *fuckin designer*. Artists are ten a fuckin penny. I'll tell you what *artists* do: stick a rabbit's foot in formaldehyde and call it Lucky."

"But you're also a writer…?"

"*Copy*writer. It's the only sort of writer people can trust these days. I sell things, mate. Keep the economy going. That's a moral imperative. Without people like me, well… I have to win the trust of the public. So. Where was I?"

"Models."

"Models. Presenters. Actresses. Models who act. Actresses who present. Presenters who model. And they look at me with those big cow eyes."

"Right."

148

"And those…" He gestured with his hands to indicate. " …udders."

"Right." Now that Ade was into farmyard metaphors, it was clear to Mel that all was not well in the Big Avocado. He could suddenly see the anguish behind the bright lights. Perhaps big money and loveless sex had started to pall for Adie. What could he do? Then he had an idea. He said: "I've got an idea."

Adie seemed surprised. He said: "*You*? What?"

"You should come back to Yorkshire where life's real. You could be happy again. There's plenty of advertising agencies in Leeds." And there really were in those days.

Adie said: "Tell me, young merkin, why would I do a fuckin stupid thing like that?"

"Because," said Mel, "you could be happy."

Adie laughed. "Happy? Like you?"

"Like me and Beatrice."

So. Mel had made his pitch – as people often said in the circles in which he moved.

BEATRICE SAID: "You better sit down. I've got some news."

Mel felt her stomach. "You're not…?"

"At my age? Perish the thought."

"Oh right. Then what… ?"

"I had a funny phone call."

Mel was outraged. "You should get on to the phone company right away. Or the phone police. I'm sure I read in the *Telegraph* there are phone police these days especially for…"

"Not that sort of call."

"What sort of call then?"

"A friend of yours. Said he was coming over to see you. To see *us*."

"Well? What's wrong with that? That's good, isn't it?"

"Ten o'clock on a Sunday morning isn't good. That's when he says he's coming. Sundays are my day of rest. I don't even look at a clean pair of knickers until well past one o'clock. Not on a Sunday."

"What's his name?"

"He's the one you met in London. The one you told me about. The artist. The one with the problems. The romantic problems. The drink problems."

"No, no, he's a designer. And a copywriter. He doesn't like being called an artist."

"He'll like whatever he gets if he comes round here on a Sunday morning. I said we could only offer him coffee. He said that was all he wanted."

"So what's he doing up here?"

"He's starting a new life. Said it's all down to you. He's got a job in Leeds with Machin & Machin."

Mel could not hide his surprise. "He took *my* advice?"

"That's the bit that scares me. There'll be some other reason we don't know about. Rape, murder, stealing a policeman's helmet..."

"Well, you'll still have to make him welcome."

"I suppose *we* will."

He could see Beatrice wasn't keen on meeting Adie, not keen at all. That was the way some married women were – jealous of their husband's friends.

"I'LL GET it!" Mel said when the doorbell rang. Then: "Beloved, this is Adie, my best friend at school."

Adie took Beatrice's hand. "He said you were beautiful but he didn't do you justice." And he kissed her on the mouth. Mel knew Adie always did that with women. None of this peck on the cheek business. He could see Beatrice didn't like it much. Eventually she pulled away.

"One of many," said Adie, "One of the many friends young Mel had in those days. Quite the centre of attention he was, this young man. None of us had any doubt that he'd get on in the world and marry a beautiful woman."

Beatrice said: "Really? We don't see many of them these days. Don't see *many* of your old schoolfriends, do we, Mel?"

Adie raised his hands in supplication to an uncaring God. "And isn't that the sadness of life? Brothers in arms in life's quest for knowledge and wisdom, we all go our separate ways in the end. *Is nothing eternal?* I often ask myself. Love, friendship, passion? The value of the pound against a basket of currencies? Why does it all run away from us? What fault is it within ourselves that allows this to happen?"

"Maybe we talk too much," said Beatrice.

Adie chuckled. "Maybe we do."

"So why did you really come back north?" Beatrice again. Mel realised he would have to give her one of his hard looks. He didn't ask his wife to like everybody *he* liked, but he did ask her to *pretend* a bit.

"I just got sick of life in the Metropolis. Truth is: those southerners don't know how to live. It's rush, rush, rush, get it done, get it done, get it done, do something else, go back to where you started, do it all again. Money, money, money. I've never been that way myself."

"*What is this life if, full of care...*"

"*...we have no time to stand and stare?*" Adie finished the line. "Mel," he said, "She's not just a beauty, is she? She knows *poetry*. She has a way with *language*."

In fact, Adie didn't stay long. After coffee and ginger biscuits he jumped to his feet. "Fortunate Mel and beautiful Beatrice, here is my fond *adieu*. Till the next time. The coffee was splendid and the company delightful." He smiled, kissed Beatrice's hand, was shown out by Mel, and disappeared up the road.

Mel called after him. "It was only instant. The coffee." And then to Beatrice: "I know you like your Sunday mornings. I know you like it if we stay in bed with the *Sunday Times*. But you could have been a bit more..."

"...willing?" She laughed. "Oh come on. You don't think *I* drove him away, do you? You don't think *that's* why he left?"

"Well..."

"You know why he came at this time, don't you? Because the pubs are shut. It's the only time he can be sure of being sober. Now it's a quarter to twelve on a Sunday morning and he's off to get pissed. He was *never* going to stay to lunch. Not even if we'd *offered*."

I do think women are very hard sometimes, thought Mel. And he wondered when they'd both get the chance to see Adie again.

IN FACT, it was only four weeks later, a Saturday night in August at a party given by the Denis Blakeneys. Mel always called Denis and Kate the Denis Blakeneys because he and Beatrice were friendly with another couple called Billy and Eloise Blakeney whom they always called the Billy Blakeneys to avoid confusion.

As soon as they had got through the front garden with its Victorian street lamp and wrought-iron bench, negotiated the front door with its brass monkey knocker, and picked up a Shiraz and a Chardonnay, sharp-eyed Beatrice said: "Isn't that your friend Adrian? Who's he with?"

Mel followed her gaze. Yes, it *was* Adie. And Mel was surprised. In fact, he'd been round alone to Adie's little *pied-a-terre* a couple of times with a small bottle of something and even met him once at Dregs – the wine bar that had once been the Nip in the Bud and would later be turned into an Oxfam shop. He didn't know that Adie knew the Denis Blakeneys but it turned out he was seeing this girl – Crystal – who was Kate Blakeney's cousin by marriage. She looked at least 15 years younger than Adie and was very pretty and blonde and wore one of those short skimpy dresses with a low neckline and spaghetti straps. "Gosh, she's nice," Mel said.

Adie saw them immediately and dragged the girl over with him. "Mel! Beatrice! Crystal! Crystal! Beatrice! Mel!" He spoke more loudly than was strictly necessary, even in the middle of a fairly noisy party crowd. He had a brandy glass in one hand but he still tried to light a cigarette with the other. It fell from his mouth and he put the lighter back in his pocket with a look of profound regret. Then he said to the girl in a slurred voice: "Here, Crystal, make yourself useful!" and handed her his glass. He turned to Mel: "You, young sir, I'll shake your hand!" And he did so. And kept on shaking it in exaggerated fashion, pump-pumping away for what seemed like ten minutes, though Mel knew it couldn't really have been that long. And then Adie seemed to tire of it all of a sudden, and he let go and leaned across to Beatrice and kissed her on the mouth, long and lingering, as he had done that Sunday morning. Mel was nonplussed. He knew Beatrice didn't like it any more than *he* liked Adie pumping his hand. But he just stood there, still and silent, until the happy return of Crystal with new supplies of Cognac eased the tension.

Mel said: "Hello, Crystal."

Crystal, who at close quarters was even more fetching in an awkward, gushy sort of way, said: "Hello. Hi. Really nice to meet you."

Adie said: "Oh, seeing you two has really made my evening, you have no idea! You have rescued me from the terrors of the cybermen. I was caught up with a clutch of computer buffs." To Beatrice he said: "Is clutch the correct collective noun for computer buffs? I know you know your stuff when it comes to the English Language..."

"It will do. Clutch will do."

"Yes, yes," said Adie, " it will *do*, lovely lady. Anyway, this clutch of morons have – sorry, has – no idea about life. That's *has* because clutch would be a singular noun. And they're all very singular people. Their notion of excitement – and I can say *their* because I am now talking about the computer crowd as individuals..."

"It doesn't matter," put in Beatrice.

"Doesn't matter?"

"I don't seriously think you want to know this. But, just for the record, a collective noun can be used as either singular or plural. You can say a crowd of drunks *is* deeply depressing or a crowd of drunks *are* deeply depressing and both statements are correct."

Mel winced. Adie turned to him. "Your wife is terrific. I hope you know how lucky you are."

Mel began to say that he *did* know how lucky he was. But Adie interrupted. "Anyway, this gaggle of gigaheads is, or are, as the case may be, comparing rival software systems in a soul-stirring quest to create the very model of a modern company account system. And that's the problem with company men – in reality, they're *no* company at all!"

Adie laughed. And, to Mel's surprise, Beatrice laughed with him.

"Well, Mrs Simmons, I never guessed you had such a beautiful laugh."

"You've never struck me as even vaguely funny before."

Mel turned to Crystal. "What did *you* think? Were you bored as well?"

"Well, I try my best, you know. I do all I can to..."

"Of course she wasn't bored," said Adie, "She loves parties. Don't you, Crystal? *Any* parties, *all* parties, the *stout* party, the *Labour* Party, the party of the first..."

Crystal turned on her heel and began to walk away but Adie reached across and grabbed her arm. "Oh, for God's sake, Crystal, what's the matter?"

She began to cry. "He doesn't take any notice of me!" she squawked. And then she ran out of the room.

"Don't walk away when I'm talking!" shouted Adie.

"Adie," said Mel, "I have to say this. You can be very rude sometimes. Yes you can." He raised a finger to emphasise his point. "You see, I may not know very much about art, or design, or collective nouns, but I do know a bit about computers. And I know enough about computers – and accounting – to know that we depend on these IT people nowadays. And that you are talking crap."

Adie put down his glass. He smiled like a little boy caught pissing on the bathroom floor. "But I carry it off, don't I? I always carry it off. Sometimes beautifully."

"Well," said Mel, "I just wonder how those computer chaps you've just been talking to in this very room maybe only five minutes ago would take your snide references now. I mean, I don't hear any computer talk at the moment so I am unable to identify who it was to whom you were talking or if they are still within earshot. You always have to be careful who might be listening. You have to be aware of what's going on around you if you want..."

And then Beatrice shouted: "*Mel, help him!*" and Adie crashed into Mel's arms. Mel struggled with the dead weight of him and Beatrice had to take Mel's glass. Beatrice said: "Get him outside."

"Yes, yes," said Mel, " Fresh air. Do him some good. Bring him round."

"Just find him some place to spew. I'll try to find the girlfriend and have a little word."

Mel stumbled to the front door, mumbling "Excuse me, excuse me" and keeping his head well down to avoid the eyes of the crowd. After what seemed like half a lifetime, he managed to get Adie out into the garden and onto the wrought-iron bench. He propped him upright then sat down beside him. Immediately Adie flopped over with his head in Mel's lap.

"Adie," said Mel, "Adie, why do you do it?"

Adie raised his head very slowly, then slumped backwards, then righted himself. He said: "Aaaaghhh!"

"Adie, you've got yourself a lovely girl there, you know that? I mean, from what I saw. Not that I know her very well. Not yet. But I could tell. A lovely girl."

"Lovely girl. Right. Too good for me. Compassionate. Cries a lot."

"And I don't know why you want to go around *offending* people. Computer people aren't evil, you know."

"Aaagghh. Software. Cyberspace. Gigabytes." A pause, then: "Intellectual property rights."

"Hey. Now you're talking. That's something I actually know a lot about..."

Adie said: "You have performed an illegal operation and your brain is about to shut down." Then he flopped over again.

"How many have you had? How long do you really think you can carry on drinking like this?"

Suddenly Adie sat bolt upright. He grinned. "Till my eyes bleed," he said.

Well, thought Mel, you're still good with words. Even at a time like this. Even in the state you're in. He was filled with a strange admiration.

Adie was violently sick over the back of the bench. Mel leapt to his feet. "Oh, why do you do it, Adie? You're such a smart fella, you've got so much going for you." Mel looked down at his trousers and was relieved to see he had escaped the vomit.

Adie slumped into unconsciousness again.

Then Beatrice appeared. She said: "I've called a taxi. There's a firm just round the corner."

"Is Crystal taking him home?"

Beatrice gave him a withering look. "Is she *fuck*! I think Crystal is a little bit shattered right now. All she could say was," and here she mimicked Crystal's voice with great accuracy, "*I tried my best, I did all I could.*" Beatrice grabbed Adie by the hair, stared disapprovingly into his face. "I ask you! Silly bitch."

"I'll go with him then. I'll go in the taxi."

"Will you *fuck*!" Beatrice let go Adie's hair and his head slumped again. "Don't forget why you're here. You've got lots of potential clients who need to be warned about the effects of the European copyright laws on next year's business plans. *You* stick to what you have to do. *I'll* get him home. Just wait till the driver gets here and you tell him the address. Nobody here is going to miss *me*."

"*I'll* miss you."

"You can always have me later."

LATER, WHEN he was back home, he rehearsed the triumphs of the evening. Two of the people he'd buttonholed had agreed he could phone them during the week and a third had made a definite appointment. But he was tired. He'd taken off his shoes and started unbuttoning his shirt before he heard the taxi sound and the key in the lock.

"God," said Beatrice, "I'm tired. That man is a big baby." She took off her dress and hung it up. "Also a big heavy lump when he's out cold like that. I don't know how you two ever got to be friends."

"You were a long time. Give you any *trouble*, did he? He didn't spew again?"

"If he had done, I'd've taken his head off with a breadknife."

"Oh, don't be so hard on him. You've not seen him at his best." He put his arms round her half-naked body, "I'd be upset if you and Adie didn't get along."

"He's a waster. That's what's so terrible – the waste. Not worth bothering about. Not worth getting caught up in. And that stupid girl – *I did all I could, but he doesn't take any notice of me!*" Her voice trailed off. "Sorry, Mel. I'm really tired. We'll do it in the morning. I promise."

So he didn't get to tell her how well he'd done. He'd have to save *that* for later too.

AFTER THAT, they didn't see much of Adie for a while. Mel could well understand why Beatrice wouldn't go near him again after all the trouble, and he didn't feel it was right to push her. But he actually heard from mutual friends that Adie was doing OK. Machin & Machin was a very respected company that produced give-away newspapers for pubs. And Adie was running the whole operation. Mel supposed it was a subject close to his heart. And a little bit later there was a new girlfriend too. So Mel decided it was time to clear the air.

"Bea," he said, "We could have them over one Sunday for dinner. Look, give him another chance, will you? This new girl – Amy – everybody says she's really great and she's been *so* good for him. He's a changed man, believe me."

"I doubt that."

"You don't know. You haven't seen him since the Denis Blakeneys. Haven't even spoken to him. Neither have *I*. I tell you he's a new man." He wore her down. And perhaps she was quite interested to see the new love in Adie's life. They finally agreed to ask Adie and Amy over for lunch the next available Sunday. This Amy was, by all accounts, pretty intelligent and taught primary school in Wakefield. "And" said Mel, "I believe she's quite a bit younger than Adie."

"My," said Beatrice, "how you do surprise me."

"You could talk to her about poetry."

"Why should I talk to her about poetry?"

"Teachers often like to talk about poetry."

"And what the fuck do *I* know about poetry?"

"Oh come on, everybody knows you know lots. Well, Adie seems to think so."

And so it came to pass. The four of them got together as Mel had planned. And Beatrice did roast beef and Yorkshire with all the trimmings followed by apple pie and custard. She was clearly making an effort to please him. And this Amy was a really pretty girl. Far more intelligent than Crystal. Anyway, it looked as if she had Adie under control. They'd brought a bottle of *Rioja* and some *After-8* mints even though it was the middle of the day

After dinner, Beatrice uncorked the wine and poured it into three glasses. Adie, to Mel's amazement, drank tonic water. And then they talked about ... oh, lots of things.

They talked about literature. "Shall I compare thee to a summer's day?" Adie asked Beatrice.

They talked about politics. "I voted for Tony Blair the first time. But I'll not vote for Gordon Brown. Not after Northern Rock," said Amy.

Business. "It's often overlooked," said Mel, "that some of the lesser known articles of the proposed European constitution will be in many ways beneficial to smaller firms in the UK. In fact, I think we're about to see a boom time for smaller businesses."

Music. "Ah," said Adie, "the food of love."

Football. "I think" said Amy, "the press was very unfair to Steve McLaren. It's no wonder he quit. And now we've got this Italian. I'm not sure I'm keen on having a foreigner. It didn't work out with Sven."

Retail oulets. "The resurgence of Marks and Spencer as a major high street player was a major surprise to many people. Still, I always refused to sell my shares," said Mel.

"Well, it's a British institution," said Amy.

Art. "Why" asked Adie, "did Picasso want to turn women into triangles? Was it an obsession with pubic hair?"

Africa. Amy blamed American foreign policy for all of it.

The credit crunch. Mel opined most of the bankers he knew really *earned* their bonuses.

When Beatrice made the coffee, Mel ambled into the kitchen. "I was right, wasn't I? This one is going to be good for him." But when the coffee was served, the talk turned to education.

"Well," said Amy, "let me tell you what it's like. Government interference. All that bloody paperwork. Ticking boxes. Filling in endless reports. Never daring to suggest that any of the pupils – sorry, the students – might be anything less than perfect. I used to *believe* in our education system, but now I wonder…"

And suddenly Beatrice waded in. "It's the teachers' fault. Because discipline's disappeared. Classes are disrupted. And examinations have become utterly corrupt. Course work, indeed! Do it once, do it twice and before we send it in, we'll get the teacher to fill in the answers. Nobody trusts teachers, nobody respects them. How can anybody work in a place where there's no discipline or trust?"

"Hey, Beatrice," said Mel, a bit alarmed by now, "I think that's pretty serious talk for Sunday afternoon."

But she couldn't be stopped. "It affects us all, doesn't it? It affects all of society. I mean, even if we don't have children…"

"Which we don't, of course. Not yet," said Mel.

"If the teachers can't get a handle on it," Beatrice went on, "the rest of us get the fallout. The crime, the unemployment! We're raising a generation of kids who don't seem to know anything, who can't see what's really going on in society."

"Which you could never say about *our* generation," put in Mel.

"What do young people know about money or making a living?" Beatrice's voice was louder now. "If it's not on Facebook, it doesn't exist. That's why we're all in trouble now – because people can't tell the difference between reality and *reality TV*. They're actually buying *debt*. Like it was something you see in an Argos catalogue. All you need to do to make a killing these days is parcel up a bunch of IOUs and flog them to the highest bidder. You take a load of shit, put it in fancy packaging, and call it an opportunity. But one thing you can't do – you can't hide the stink."

But Amy hit back. "You can't blame teachers for the failures of society. It's the financial system that's at fault. Here we are, shovelling money into the banks to keep them afloat and the bankers are still creaming off their bloody bonuses. It's…"

Beatrice turned to Adie. "What do *you* think? Be honest now."

There was a pause, then a general silence. For once, Adie appeared surprised, at a loss. For once, no instant aphorism gathered on his lips. He looked round, tapped a fingernail against his glass of tonic water and said: "What do *I* think? Well, I think if you have capitalism, you'll always have recession. It's like with religion. If you have religion, you've got to have hell. You can't have one without the other." And then, as though catching himself being boringly serious, he lurched into joviality. "Hey, Mel, young business brain of the year, at least *one* of us is still doing well. I hear you've got lots of new contracts out of this European legislation stuff. Half a dozen was what I heard. So *somebody's* still living off the fat of the land, thank God."

"Well, yes," said Mel, "I have. I'm glad you mentioned that, Adie. On the night of the Denis Blakeneys' party, I got a strong hint from you that you found my line of work fairly uninteresting." Then he paused. "How did you *know* I'd got lots of new contracts?"

There was another pause. Then Adie said: "I don't know. Someone must have told me."

"Well, not many people knew..."

Beatrice interrupted. "I might have told a couple of people..."

"Yes," said Adie quickly, "and those people must have told *me*. These things get around. Success stories always do in times of uncertainty. Spread like wildfire."

Mel was all smiles. "Well, that's my wife for you. She's always supportive, always proud of the things I do. Marriage is a great thing, you know." He almost winked at Amy, but thought better of it.

"Yes," said Adie.

"Trust," said Mel, "Stability. Something to build your life on. I'd recommend it to anybody."

And Amy suddenly looked across at Mel and said "You really never knew, did you? You *really* never knew...!"

"...just how much we follow your career!" said Adie and laughed. Then, for some reason, everybody laughed. And the ill feeling of just a few minutes ago was gone.

Afterwards, when they were stacking the plates, Mel said to Beatrice: "I think that went really well. Well, I think it went *allright*. Certainly nothing *less* than allright. And did you see Adie's driving them home? I don't think I've ever seen him drive anybody home from a party before."

"Hardly a *party*."

"Well, you *were* a bit aggressive during the Great Education Debate. Maybe next time you'll go a little easier on the girl."

"I don't think there'll *be* a next time. I don't think she's the one for him." She closed the door of the dishwasher and pressed the starter.

AND BEATRICE was right. When Mel bumped into Crystal Blakeney at Dregs – she'd started going out with a chap from his office – she told him Adie and Amy were no longer an *item*, as she put it. She said Adie had been in the bar on his own one night going through a re-run of his routine about women being too good for him – and a new something-or-other about how he didn't deserve to have any *friends* either.

Then, ten days later, Adie was dead.

The inquest said *open verdict* because they couldn't be sure whether Adie jumped from the top floor of the car park or just fell off, considering all the booze inside him. But Mel couldn't figure it out. Why would Adie kill himself? OK, his big romance had broken up. But he'd been through that sort of thing before and he'd always got over it. On the other hand, Machin & Machin had gone into liquidation because of all the pubs that were closing down. So maybe the threat of losing his job was part of it.

The coroner said it was a blessing Adie hadn't been able to get to his car, which meant other lives might well have been saved. Mel thought that was pretty unfeeling. He suddenly remembered that thing Adie had said to him once: *The ground broke my fall.* He was always good at little phrases that stuck in the mind.

Even Beatrice was put out by Adie's death, and cried a lot, which surprised him. He thought it was a shame she'd never got to know him better.

It was a funny old life. A talented chap like Adie who had everything – brains, looks, charm – he just couldn't cut it.

But an ordinary bloke like Mel, who married a good wife, ended up happy and fulfilled.

He tried to say this to Beatrice, to sort of thank her for everything. He said: "I want you to know I'll always be here for you. Just as *you'll* always be here for *me*."

And it was lovely. She just smiled and said: "Till my eyes bleed."

Now It Can Be Told

I WAS in Dallas four hours after the shooting. That plane journey was rough. I spent the whole time trying not to think about what had happened – reading some sci-fi magazine I picked up at La Guardia.

Anyway, when I got there, I very nearly didn't get to see him. I was out in the hospital lobby, talking to a security man – one of those joes with five o'clock shadow and no forehead that people like Hoover and Helms liked to recruit because they'd seen them in the movies. And he was clucking over my ID, glancing from the card to my face and back again. Maybe he thought I would suddenly break down from the weight of his dead eyes alone, and admit I was some undercover reporter for the *Dallas Tribune* or a hit-man for Chairman Mao.

"Mar-vin Jones," he said, tasting each syllable with deep suspicion, "Committee for Government Research."

"Chairman," I said.

"Huh?"

I couldn't believe he said "huh" but I said it again: "Chairman. Of the Committee."

"Never heard of it," he said and handed me my wallet back.

These guys never got through sixth grade but they still figure if they never heard of it, it doesn't exist. I didn't know what to say next. I'd already told him Jack was expecting me and he'd just grinned and turned down my polite suggestion that he made the necessary phone call. "Look, bub," he said, "Maybe you didn't hear the news. The President got shot today and he's still coming round. Only family and top people – I *mean* top people – get to come through here. The guy's got a bullet in his shoulder, for God's sake!" He shouted the last bit and shrugged and mugged for the crowd. They glanced round appreciatively, all those rubberneckers. They were bored.

And I didn't want to make a fuss out there in public, with reporters and photogs hanging around.

And then I had a stroke of look. Julie Goodall, one of Jackie's people, came out of the elevator, like the goddess out of the machine, and she looked round and saw me and came on over.

"Hi, Marv," she said. This Julie was blonde and a looker and the fact of having the President shot and the Governor of Texas killed all in one day hadn't phased her enough to dent her Max Factor routine. She still looked great. She didn't even glance at the joe with the shadow. "Let him through, Ezra," she said.

He looked like he was going to spit but stopped himself and stepped aside. Max Factor had won through again. "OK, Miss Goodall."

"*Ezra*," I said quietly as I walked past him into the elevator.

"*Mar-vin*," he said and made farting noises with his lips.

In the elevator, I grabbed Julie's breast and kissed her hard and she said: "Oh, Marv!" sort of meltingly, like she might almost give a damn. But then she got hold of herself almost as fast as I had. She said: "He's fine, just fine. Fuckin miracle. I hope they get the guy and burn his balls."

"How's Jackie?" I didn't like the notion of having any hysterics around me in the next half hour and she was the only one who might go that way.

"No problem. A shot in the arm and a spot of shut-eye. Naturally, she's got a private room. And a big space to hang Christian Dior."

Upstairs a ward had been duly emptied for the injured President. The first shock was over, the medics had moved aside and the people round Kennedy – the secretaries, the gophers, the bodyguards and the fixers – were too professional to let the trauma get to them. And, of course, they were relieved, oh so relieved. They still had a President and they still had jobs. So the Governor of Texas was laid out on a slab in the Dallas morgue? So what? He was fixing to lose an election anyway. The Connolly people – his family and hangers-on – were all over the city, mourning their loss. But Jack Kennedy was alive and kicking and the rest of the country was *joyous*. Joyous enough for a second term, for God's sake.

We went down a corridor and through a white door and there he was with a swell-looking nurse in a 42 bra leaning over

164

him and two security men looking kind of sheepish. He was sat in a red-and-blue striped armchair wearing a green and gold dressing gown with his right arm in a sling and he looked every inch the hero except he was a shade paler than usual. He grinned when he saw me – the famous white flash – and stretched out his left hand to grip mine. "Marv," he said.

"Mr President," I said. I was always formal in company. "How's the shoulder?"

He touched the sling with his left hand. "A scratch – believe me." He even *sounded* like the hero of a movie. "You want a glass of milk?" he said, "It's all they got here."

"Thanks, but I'll pass."

He motioned me to sit down on a canvas-and-tubular-steel chair opposite. "OK, Joe Friday, who did it? And how come we didn't know they were gonna try?"

"In front of all these people?"

He waved his good arm. "All you people, take a powder. Marv and I have some talking to do." The security men made off right away, as did Julie. But the nurse hesitated. Jack gave her one of those smiles. "Sorry to be so abrupt, honey. National security is at stake." He raised a finger to his lips and kissed it slowly and she smiled back to show she understood and followed the others out the door.

"Two words," I said when the door closed, "Sam Giancana."

"Shit," he said. Then he nodded. "It makes the best sense."

"The Mob don't like you, Jack, not any more. Giancana took a risk when he got them to bankroll you. I guess he did it for your dad's sake." I paused to let him take it in. "Oh come on now, even Hoover knows about your old man running booze for Capone. It's history."

"Not in the schools in *my* state," he said.

"I guess your dad convinced Sam that things would be hunky-dory with *his* boy in the White House. But you didn't play by their rules."

"That little Bobby is a whippersnapper sure enough." Jack grinned again. Maybe it was post-gunshot-wound euphoria, but he was in a good mood.

165

"It was *you* made him attorney general."

"And he's doing a good job."

"Nobody said he *wasn't*. In fact, that's Giancana's main complaint. Also," I hesitated but decided I ought to be straight about everything I knew, "There's a personal thing here too. You fucked Giancana's girl. Now she's dead, Sam blames you."

That shook him. A little. The grin disappeared.

I said: "It's my job to know these things." And it was. Ever since Jack created the Committee for Government Research and made me Chairman. It was my job to spook the spooks, check out what the CIA and the FBI and the Department of Justice really knew and how they were fixing to use it.

Jack said: "You're right. I should never have messed with that little whore. I don't even like her movies. I blame Sinatra. He told me how good she was."

"Giancana blames Sinatra too. I hear he sent him a sheep's head. The joke on Sunset Boulevard is when Sinatra sings *Someone to Watch Over Me*, he really needs it."

"Maybe *I* need it too. It's your job to know these things. That's what you just said, Marv. So how come they got this close?"

I hesitated just long enough to let him know he'd got to me. "There's some high involvement. You could say the usual channels – the people we normally depend on – were bypassed."

"You're talking CIA." It wasn't a question.

I spread my hands. That was exactly who I meant. "You ever hear of Lee Harvey Oswald?"

"Sounds like a New England law firm. But no, I never heard of him."

"I think you're about to."

A DAY later and everybody had heard of Oswald. We were sitting in the Oval office and Jack was back in a suit and tie, pouring the Scotch with his left hand. I made myself as comfortable as I could on the black leather couch, knowing that Jackie would be mad if there were any alcohol stains, while Jack took up his favourite position – at the big desk underneath the American Eagle. He always looked like the guy in charge but never as much as he did behind that desk. Twenty-four hours with eight hours' solid sleep in there had done him the world of good. The tan looked natural again and even the sling suited him in a battered Bogart sort of way.

I heard Mrs JFK still had the heebie-jeebies but I wasn't going to ask. I said: "In the first place, we don't believe he's the guy who pulled the trigger."

"So tell me what we *do* believe."

"The Dallas PD picked him up pretty fast. He took one of them out in the process. Allegedly. No witnesses to that. Now this Oswald was already down on everybody's books as a Commie through and through. Loves the Russkis. He's even married to a Russian woman."

"But…"

"But he gets around too easily. He just hops on planes to Moscow, Havana…"

"So he's got friends in high places, so he's a double working for somebody over here?"

I sighed and took a drink. "I think nobody knows, not even Oswald. Look, Jack, this guy's a fantasist. He even made a record, an LP. Paid for it himself. I kid you not. I've been giving it a listen in the line of duty. Deaf man's Perry Como." I let the whisky slosh around in my mouth a while. It was Tomatin, 12 years old, the real stuff. "Oswald is one of those lost souls that bounce around like pinballs, scoring points for one side or the other. I guess he trades information when he's got it, but that isn't often. I guess both sides are still waiting for him to do something useful then they can claim him for their own. One thing's for sure – now the cops have got him, he won't cut too much ice with Krushchev."

I thought I'd let Jack have a minute or two to mull things over but I could see he was already ahead of the game.

"So somebody – somebody in the CIA – figures he's a natural patsy. Giancana's man pulls the trigger and the CIA has Oswald there to take the fall. Commie bastard. Hates America. Giancana's out of the frame." He thought about it a moment. "But when he gets into court…" He gave me the chance to finish his sentence but I didn't bother so he did it himself. "This guy Oswald isn't going to make it into any court, is he, Marv?"

"If it was me, I wouldn't let him."

"If it was me, I wouldn't either. How's it gonna happen?"

"The Dallas PD keep bringing him out to show the reporters and the rubber-neckers how smart they've been. My thinking is somebody is gonna stand in the middle of the crowd, maybe wearing one of those PRESS stickers on his hat like you see on TV, and just take a pot-shot. All those Texas boys carry 38s when they go to the opera anyway. *Grand ol'* opera, that is."

"So. Somebody shoots Oswald and Sam is in the clear."

"*Everybody's* in the clear. Nobody makes the Mafia connection."

We both thought about that.

"The guy who does it will be a patriot. Some kind of hero," said Jack.

"Bound to make parole in three to five years."

"I take it you're not planning to interfere."

"It's not my jurisdiction, Jack. Police matter, that's all."

And we both laughed. Damn, that Scotch was good.

I DIDN'T see Jack for a few weeks after that, though we talked a lot on the phone after Ruby pulled the trigger. We thought at one stage the Warren Commission might be a problem but Jack made sure Bobby was involved from the start. And when the election came up the following year, Jack was so far ahead in the polls that the Republicans didn't even try. They put up that crazy Goldwater and Jack took everywhere except Dixieland and Arizona, Goldwater's home state.

And everybody knows what happened next. They know about the Civil Rights Bill that made sure Dixieland came back to us – with *black* votes this time. About the second Bay of Pigs invasion which took Castro out of the picture and into exile in a Moscow coldwater apartment. About the Non-Proliferation Treaty with the Russians that made sure Israel didn't get the Bomb.

Of course, there were some things people didn't like about Jack's second term. They didn't like him pulling our military advisers out of Viet Nam so Ho Chi Minh could just sail in and take over, but then they didn't have any idea how bad things could have got over there.

Even so, they still elected Bobby to continue Jack's work in '68. And it was Bobby who really turned the heat on the Mafia then, so everybody remembers the Grand Jury hearings and the trials that saw the Five Families behind bars for a generation. And people still ask about how Giancana died, though the conventional wisdom is somebody from the Gotti family took him out with a Kalazhnikov before he could turn state's evidence. Myself, if somebody asks me, I say what all those bastards used to say: *I'm pleading the fifth.*

When Jack became Ambassador to Russia, lots of people thought it was a gimmick. But Jack had got really close to Krushchev by that time and it was this as much as the Special Trade Agreement that convinced the old bear to take on the rest of the Kremlin and start up those *glasnost* policies that freed Eastern Europe.

So. Letting Oswald take that bullet was a small price to pay.

The last time I saw Jack was two weeks before the turn of the century and three days before his death in the Mary Mother of God Hospital which the Kennedys had built at Hyannis Port. His mind was going by then, as everybody knew, though most people believed the stroke story and the Catholic staff were suitably discreet about any mention of AIDS. He still had his lucid moments and we managed to talk pretty cogently about the old times. That's when I told him about this story I'd read in one of my sci-fi magazines. It was something called a *contrafactual* – which is a fancy word for history that never happened. Like, it supposed Jack had been killed that day in Dallas and Connolly was the one who'd only been wounded.

We were sitting on reclining chairs in his private ward. He was wearing a white towelling robe and pouring the Perrier water with both hands – booze was strictly *verboten*. "We should have your old man here today," I told him and he laughed and showed the old Jack teeth again. Then I told him about the story. "Imagine," I said, "it's *you* lying on that slab and the vultures gather…"

He nodded to show he was paying attention.

169

"There's old LBJ in the White House and he just gets bogged down in Viet Nam and pretty soon we've got 20,000 troops out there…"

He laughed out loud at that.

"And the country is torn apart between the military and the goddamn pacifist left and there's marches and protests and terrorist groups…"

"What happened to Castro?"

"Fidel stays in power for 30 years…"

He laughed again. "And who won the '68 election?"

"Nixon gets to win the '68 election."

He pretty much choked on that one. "Why, that bastard was finished for sure after I took care of him. He was *never* gonna come back until Hell froze over."

"At least the guy who wrote it knew what Nixon was really like. In *his* version the creep gets caught out in some slush fund scandal and only stays out of jail by making a deal and resigning."

"Now that *does* sound like Nixon. Except he'd get his dog to resign instead."

Then we got to talking about what really might have happened if Sam's man had been a better shot and we decided things might have been pretty bad. But not *that* bad.

And the point I'm making – now that my Captain is dead and nothing can touch him – is something for all those do-gooders and moral busybodies and bleeding heart liberals who voted for the Kennedys but didn't like the methods they used. And didn't like the low-life they mixed with. And didn't like the fact they fucked so many women.

It's just this: *You have to live in the real world.*

OK. That's it. I'm all through now.

About the author

Michael Yates was successively reporter and film critic on the Sheffield Star newspaper, and also worked as a subeditor for the Bradford Telegraph and the Huddersfield Examiner.

He freelanced as a theatre critic for the Yorkshire Evening Post and taught playwriting at Harrogate Theatre and creative writing for the Workers Educational Association. In 2010 he was Writer in Residence in Bradford Schools.

He has had short stories published in magazines and anthologies and won short story prizes from the Jersey Arts Centre, The Armagh Writers Festival and the Wolds Words Festival. Michael has been Poet in Residence in Whitby, in Wakefield Hospitals and at Wakefield Cathedral and has published three volumes of verse.

Twelve of Michael's plays have been performed in the North of England, including Manchester, Leeds and Bradford. One of his plays, *Life Sentence*, won the Stanley Arnold Trophy at the Sheffield One-Act Play Festival in 2009. And another, *Sunday Afternoon Again*, was chosen for Liverpool's Write Now Drama Festival in 2012.

Also by Michael Yates in Nettle Books

Life Class

A collection of more than 90 poems about life, love and plenty of other things that don't even alliterate! *"Delight in the careful observations and appreciate the wisdom of the depictions, for reading this book is truly a life class"* – John Irving Clarke in his introduction.
£9.95. ISBN 978-0-9561513-0-8

The Bronte Boy

In this tragic drama, young Branwell, who once ruled an imaginary childhood world, is now a man, grown mad trying to cope with the *real* one. Having failed as a poet and painter, as doomed in love as he is in literature, he slips ever more quickly down the road of drink, drugs and despair. His loving father Patrick and talented sister Charlotte fight a last-ditch stand for his sanity; but it is Branwell's sinister friend, gravedigger John Brown, who threatens to have the last word.
£6. ISBN 978-0-9561513-1-5

Short Shorts

Three one-act plays – *Life Sentence, Till My Eyes Bleed* and *Sunday Afternoon Again*. Full text and cast & Crew.
£6. ISBN 978-0-9561513-3-9

Also in Nettle Books

Flying with a Broken Wing

By Sat Mehta

Flying with a Broken Wing tells the true story of a boy growing up in India in turbulent times.

Sat Mehta was five years old when he and his family became refugees, caught up in the biggest migration in modern history at the time of Independence. His home was destroyed, his uncle murdered. Once very wealthy farmers, the Mehtas became destitute.

Later, Sat suffered a broken arm – complications set in and amputation seemed inevitable. As he lay in hospital, a world famous surgeon, Professor Robert Roaf, strode onto the ward, choosing "hopeless cases" to help. Sat got a second chance.

The gratitude he felt for the great man's skill shaped the rest of Sat's life. He qualified as a doctor and arrived in England, where he has lived and worked for 30 years.

He says of his life: "It is a story of a disappearing world, sadhus, snakes and baking sun, monkeys, monsoons and riot and murder. As a boy, I saw it all."

£10. ISBN 978-0-9561513-2-2

www.ingramcontent.com/pod-product-compliance
Lightning Source LLC
Chambersburg PA
CBHW020617250626
47154CB00004B/1544